THE HIGH ALIVE

AN EPIC HOODOO DIPTYCH

THE UTTERANCES

The 3rd Thing 2020 Cohort

Juan Alonso-Rodríguez | 2020 Cover Artist
Ink and graphite drawings from Cuban-born artist Juan Alonso-Rodríguez's *Palm Desert* series reflect the influence on his work of "the organized balance, pattern and symmetry found in nature."

Melissa Bennett | 2020 Land Acknowledgment Writer
The poems that appear at the front of each 2020 title are offered by Indigenous poet Melissa Bennett "as medicine across generations."

Jennifer Calkins | Fugitive Assemblage
California, 1983. A woman pulls an IV out of her arm, walks out of the hospital, and starts driving north. *Fugitive Assemblage* is lyric noir rendered through ghostly images and voices conjured out of the trauma of family, of place, of love.

Marilyn Freeman | The Illuminated Space: A Personal Theory & Contemplative Practice of Media Art
Expansive and personal, lyrical and analytical, fragmented and fluent, *The Illuminated Space* divines the dialectical nature of time-based art.

Megan Sandberg-Zakian | There Must Be Happy Endings: On a Theater of Optimism & Honesty
An artistic coming-of-age story in ten essays, *There Must Be Happy Endings* navigates the ethics of making hopeful art in an unjust and chaotic world.

Carlos Sirah | The High Alive: An Epic Hoodoo Diptych
The Light Body and *The Utterances* transform book into performance space for a mythopoesis of blackness and queerness, of return and foray in this tête-bêche diptych of grief and possibility.

The 3rd Thing is an independent press dedicated to publishing necessary alternatives. Each year we produce a suite of projects that represents our interdisciplinary, intersectional priorities in terms of form, content and perspective. We think of these projects as a cohort in conversation with one another and readers, contributing to our endeavor to create not just beautiful books, but culture.

"The third thing" is the idea that emerges when we use imagination instead of compromise to solve a problem, meet a need, resolve a conflict, answer a question, question an answer, get where we're going, go somewhere new.

the3rdthing.press

THE HIGH ALIVE

AN EPIC HOODOO DIPTYCH

THE UTTERANCES

Carlos Sirah

The 3rd Thing, Olympia, Washington

Acknowledgments

I'm thankful for the many collaborations in life and art. Deep wells of gratitude to my family – the living and the dead – Corinne, Sally, Betty and Ollie, Joe Sam and Anna Mae, Elizabeth, Delores, Mae Fannie, Meadie, Sherry, Gwen – who thread and hold family. To my parents, Rose and Gene, for life and battle. Thank you to my siblings, Brittany and Kendrick, for sustained acts of conspiracy. To a multitude of cousins who are like siblings. To my grandmother Ora, for groundwork.

A profound thanks to the artists who helped me see this work in its many iterations: Mauricio Salgado, Victor Nasir Terry, Andrew Colarusso, Ronald Kevin Lewis, Cherise Morris, Sophia Rowler, Marina McClure, Darby James Davis, Kyra Riley, Danté Jeanfelix, Ryan Johnson, Isabelle Pierre, Ashton Muñiz, Marcus Jones, Adenike Thomas, Damian Joel, Anthony Franqui, and Deanna Supplee.

Tremendous thanks to my many teachers, from whom I continue to learn: Mrs. Lake, Mrs. Micou, Dawn Akemi Saito, Aimee Meredith Cox, Daniel Alexander Jones, Erik Ehn, Paula Vogel, Lisa D'amour, Sharon Bridgforth.

A divine thanks to my friends, the holy unsettlers, who hold space for experimentation in life, which is art: I continue to learn from you: Diane Exavier, Dalia Taha, Arielle Julia Brown, Ashley Teague, Reginald Taylor, David Barclay Moore, Amen Igbinosun, Erik Ruin, Susie Husted, Cherise Morris, Juan Miguel Spinnato, Jordana Delacruz, Gabriel Payan, Susie Husted, Ary Lavallee, Akilah Walker, Rima Mahmoud, and Vida Mia Ruiz, and Katie KaVang.

I thank the architects of thought and road, whom I've attempted to write alongside: Colin Dayan, John Keene, Saidiyah Hartman, Fred Moten, Sarah Ahmed, Kiese Laymon, Ashon Crawley, Art Ensemble of Chicago, Essex Hemphill, Christina Sharpe, Nathaniel Mackey, Anne Carson, Toni Morrison, Adrienne Kennedy, Brian Turner,

Louise Glück, Omi Osun Jones, Wilson Harris, Yusef Komunyakaa, and so many more.

Thank you to the many residencies that provided space and shelter for this work: Virginia Center for Creative Arts, The Hambidge Center, Blue Mountain Center, Millay Colony, MacDowell Colony, and Lamda Literary.

Thanks to my veteran community for the difficult and thankless work of articulating possibility amid perpetual war: Warrior Writers, About Face (Iraq Veterans Against the War), Veteran Art Movement, and an especial thanks to Lovella Calica, for your steadfastness.

Notes

The Light Body considers, then, permutates this line from the poet Paul Éluard – *There is another world, but it is inside this one.*

The Utterances owes a considerable debt to Zora Neale Hurston and her work and documentation in *Characteristics of Negro Expression.*

for the living and the dead

In theory. *We.* Conjure body. One thousand years. Autochthonous spirits. Ride sound. Towards body. Of woven nerve. Of shattered mind. Of high and blessed and holy duration. By mean and time. Of the radiant flesh. By blessed tongues. Sung and unheard. Reprieve then, the flatted fifth, not the war horn.

In the night. Among the many thousand breaths. Expire and Inspire. Of Her. Of Bessie. Assemblage. Itself. Torn apart, Bessie's breath. Shreds. The night. In return. Be bodied.

The night.

Asks you. Who hides? Beneath music. Dream. Let Bessie. Inside. We fail in silence. Bessie's breath hovers. About your bed. Again. Your fear. Being. The same. You go. Migration. Your body. You cannot. We fail. Stutter. Vacation. Your body. No yield. Your heart. Would leap. Out. Holy breath. Of Bessie. Ask. When is safety?

The war horn. Not. The flatted fifth. Please. Window open. Breath vacates. Tonight. Rest. Open your mouth. Fill. Your mouth. Be filled with sound. Bessie's breath. With us. Bessie. Breath. Defeated. Linear hordes. Imperial. Longing. Sound. Regather. Sound.

One thousand years ago. We leave.

The city.

Remember.

The night.

NIGHT ONE | gather

Theory of Bessie—cults of fragment, heralds of possibility, interpreters of remnant, gather us in festival. Together. Each theory within Theory of Bessie converges, processing down foothills, into valley, where you listen and wait.

To witness.

Theory of Bessie instantiate the recollected city.

After all that has happened. The exile. The return.

The War that Settled Dust.

One thousand years. *Eighty-five trillion breaths.* Theory of Bessie loved and salvaged sacred grain.

Theory of Bessie shout and praise. Each theory within Theory of Bessie revels in their sound. Theory of Bessie revel in the sounded body. Theory of Bessie is Body. Their manner and shape. Holy.

Each theory bears stalk upon dried stalk of the grain who is endurance and makes possible endurance. Call the grain *Maize-Maize.*

Theory of Bessie sound their bodies down from the foothills bare-chested, loose-footed, in garments of hued sound gathered in the years since the long war. They wear raiment colored and sounded in sumac or indigo or lichen or bloodroot with skin covered or painted or free to the night. The night smells of kyphi and kopal and hickory and pine.

Theory of Bessie bear earthen vessels of water. Theory of Bessie bear sound. They bear wood and iron. Some theories bear arms of *Maize-Maize.* Hear the cacophony of the multitude. Theory of Bessie sound against Catastrophe.

Their number, in the thousands, reaches the field in the valley where you wait and listen with the others. You hear their sound before their body arrives.

Theory of Bessie stream into the valley.

Behold, the multitude of the living!

Theory of Bessie settle into the valley. Onto the field. The clearing. That ritual space. Theory of Bessie spiral about the field. Their heads bent to the hills from where they come or bent towards the ground where you sit and listen and witness and wait and listen and sit and listen. Together.

Theories unsettle dust, while the multitude theories shape into space.

Listen.

Theory of Bessie place the stalks on the field which is a threshing floor, which is the ritual space or the space of possibility or the space before the sound or the dimension of encounter.

Theory of Bessie arrange the vessels of cast iron in the ritual space. Theory of Bessie fill the large iron vessels with water. Theories pour and pour into vessel upon vessel. Water.

Theory of Bessie take in breath. As one. As these theories settle into this valley, so do other theories settle into other valleys across the lands.

Those who would tell the story, keen and exalt. The flatted fifth, not the war horn. Theory of Bessie unsettles story.

Those who will tell the story do. Theory of Bessie performs.

A city emerges.

THE CITY

You are inside the city. Listen closely. More even than that. Better. Listen like this.

Hear fugitives carry weight inside the city. Naif, an innocent, with Rebl, some species of outlaw, carry the weight of a body through the streets of the city. It is quiet. Except. Hear their worn soles collide into rubble. Hear them travel across whole city blocks. Hear the empty sack as it slides across Rebl's calloused back. Hear how the weight of the body is at times so great that Naif drops a leg.

Holy thud.

When Naif and Rebl reach down to catch the one leg, the other drops. The knees of the taller one buckle. They would move together. So, they have carried this body for whole city blocks. They must not forget to breathe.

Naif and Rebl slow. Stutter before one another, for the task to carry weight is not, even after all that has happened, insignificant. Hear them listen. The shorter of the duo slows. Rebl stutters before his companion. Listens across the distance of a body. Rebl and Naif breathe together. Naif and Rebl return to the body with more determination. They assess the weight of the body and they move as by seesaw, weight shifting from one and then to the other, with the body, until they can slowly and carefully place the body upon the ground. The body, at first, does not move. The body catches, freezes, resting in a state not unlike rigor mortis. The body collapses onto the ground.

The body catches again. Naif and Rebl scurry.
The body catches, gasps, moans, collapses.

Into death?

GASP GASP

MOAN

MOAN CATCH

CATCH COLLAPSE

Naif and Rebl stutter.

Naif and Rebl return to the body.

Rebl
Fuck!

MOAN
MOAN
CATCH

Naif
This body fucking reeks.

MOAN
MOAN

Rebl
Shut up!

Naif
What?

Rebl
You been singing that same tired ass song for whole city blocks.
You act like you never smelled flesh before.

Naif
Could be a man.

Rebl
It is a man.
What else would it be on these streets?

Naif
Tall.

Rebl
...but what kind of man?

Naif
But not too tall.

Rebl
Do you think he was a soldier?

Naif
If he was, then you know we should've left them.
Aww. It's gone be in my clothes!

Rebl
It could be one of us.

Naif
One of us?

Rebl
Yeah, you know...escaped, on the loose, on the run, running.

Naif
I'm'onna be smelling like this for weeks.

Rebl
It's not like you were smelling like gardenias before.

Naif

I don't know what you talking bout.
I wash in the reservoir by the factory.

Rebl

All the way over there?
It's not a factory.
Nothing gets made there.

Naif

One of the few places that gets quiet.
I never hear any explosion over there.
What's a gardenia?

Rebl

That's right.
You smell like that reservoir.
Don't worry about what they are.
Just know you don't smell like them.

Naif

Okay.

Rebl

You smell like by-product.

Naif

Okay.

Rebl
Cause that's what the reservoir smell like.

Naif
I said okay!
I thought we were gonna be friends.

Rebl
Can he speak?

Naif
Dunno.

Rebl
Figure it out.

Naif
Why I gotta figure it out?

Rebl
Cause if you don't figure, and you take the wrong bones…
You'll end up right back in that cell, or worse.

Naif goes over to the body, surveys the body totally. After careful study, Naif lowers himself before the body.

Naif
Can you speak?
into the body's ear, whispering at first inquiry, then love, then frustration.
Can you speak? Can you speak?
What if it's a she?

Rebl
Why would it be a she?

GASP GASP
MOAN
MOAN CATCH

CATCH COLLAPSE

Rebl
Don't sound like no she to me.

Naif
We shouldn't have come back to the city.
We should've stayed at the prison.

Rebl
And what, starve?
If we didn't leave, we wouldn't get work.
If we don't work, we don't eat, or worse,
And you don't want worse.

Naif surveys the body.

Naif

Shit shit shit shit shit shit shit.

Rebl

Now, don't be nervous.
So, have you made a determination?

Naif

I think it's definitely a man.
Or definitely a woman.
Or definitely a human.

Rebl

All dummies come from...
Wait. Where are you from?

STUTTER

Naif

You didn't say she'd be alive.

Rebl

Obviously, I didn't know that did I?
You know you'll have to look?
I'll make you a wager.
And stop saying she.

Naif

Nope nope nope nope nope nope.
It'll be like last time.

theories draw closer to Naif and Rebl

Rebl

Man, woman, specials, dogs…
What's it going to be?

Naif

You won't pay.

Rebl

I'll pay you.
I'll give you my shirt.

Naif

Your shirt smells like mine.

Rebl

But looka here.
What's that?
Smell it.

Naif

Oh, it smells good.

Rebl
This shirt smell fresh, don't it?

Naif
You didn't the last time.

Rebl removes the sack from his back. Opens it.

Rebl
Look inside.
Is this sack full?

STUTTER

Rebl
Well is it?

Naif
No.

Rebl
No, it's not.
And if we don't fill this sack,
You know what's gonna happen?

Naif
We're gonna starve.

Rebl
Worse. You'll end up in this sack. Is that what you want?

Naif
But things are different now.

Rebl
It's gon' have to be full. Or the one who grinds.
He's gonna laugh and not weigh.

Naif
You didn't pay me!

Rebl
Why you bring up old shit?

Naif
No no no no. You won't pay.

Rebl
Different rules.
We're closer now.
To tell the truth,
I didn't know if I could trust you.
And besides, we not in prison no more.

Naif
Nuh uh. You Tricky.

Rebl
I'll pay.
I promise.
I will pay.

Naif
How?

Rebl
Remove the clothing.

Naif
But, what if you win?

Rebl
If I win. If I win?
If I win…

Naif
Yes. I won the last time.
You didn't pay.
You might win this time.
I want to know what I have to lose if you win.

Rebl
You have to promise
to work
with me to find other
others
This won't be the last
sack.
Deal?

Naif
Other bodies?

Rebl
Yes, bodies!
Where are you from!

Naif
Okay!

Rebl
Okay.

Naif
Okay…But for how long?

Rebl
I guess 'til you win a bet. Okay?

STUTTER

Rebl
Get to it then.

STUTTER

Rebl
Do something.

Naif lowers himself. Places ear to body. Naif listens.

Naif

What are you? What are you?
What are you?
Who are you?

Rebl

You think he's gonna talk
to you
looking like that?

Naif

But there's not even any skin left.
I can't even tell what the skin is
Was.

Rebl

A bet is a bet is a bet
is a bet is a bet
How good is your word?

Naif

Let me use your blade.

Rebl

I don't have a blade.
Use your hands.

Naif tries to rip the clothing with hands. It doesn't happen.

Naif
I'ma need something sharp. Let me get the blade.

Rebl
You got teeth, dontcha?

Naif
Nuh uh…I won't.
I ain't doing that.

Rebl
I knew it.
Your word is nothing.
You know what? You are nothing. Yeah. You are nothing. Go ahead, say it with me. You are nothing. You. Are. Nothin-

Naif
You are noth—I'm not saying that.

Rebl
What are you? Hmph. You ever been anything?

Naif
Okay okay okay okay okay.

Naif lowers himself to the body.
Teeth Rends Cloth

GASP MOAN CATCH COLLAPSE

Naif
Fuck fuck fuck fuck fuck fuck fuck.

MOAN MOAN
MOAN MOAN
MOAN

Rebl
You know what?
Fuck this shit!
I'm gonna eat.

Rebl picks up a large stone.

Naif
What are you doing?

Rebl
We're gonna eat!

Naif
No!

Naif places himself between the body and Rebl.

theories
beat
the ground,
unsettling
dust

Rebl

You better get outta my way.

Naif

No. You owe. Me. You owe me. I said no. You owe me.
I let you out.

Rebl places himself over the body. Rebl drops the stone.
Naif holds the body.
Naif and the body breathe as one.

A body can be. Altared burning. There's a way. *Do you remember?* The sound… *It journeys.* Down. Centuries. We witnessed ash. Bombs fell. On bodies. We shouted. Dust settled. Onto skin. We moaned. Dust settled. We praised. Daylight. We waited. Dust settled. Have you been burned?

Beyond shape.
Beyond sound.

A body can. Be covered. People do. Dust settles. Onto furniture. Onto windows. Onto limbs.

Beyond the sound.
Beyond the listening.

A body can be. Recovered. People get rags. People. Dust people move. On about. The work. Of living. Every time. Unsettling dust. Sending. Dust back. Into air. Breathe dust. In the body. Again. We were not fugitive by choice but by nuclear declaration.

Forget the body. Raise the dead. Only. Do battle.

Dust will settle.

Rejoice.

NIGHT TWO | split

Theory of Bessie gather wood brought from the woods of the foothills. Theory of Bessie split pine and oak and sweetgum. They breathe fire into wood beneath the cast iron vessels.

The air be filled with wood.

Water. All the night, Theory of Bessie fill and refill the cast iron. Pouring. All the night, Theory of Bessie wait and listen. Until. Within a perfect pocket of sound. When the wood splits. Scent and ash. Of pine and oak and sweetgum. Waft across the valley. A voice is heard.

An echo of sermon.
Vapor frees itself.
You can hear them.
Feint.

One voice.

Splitting.

Many bodies.

CHURCH

Inside the church ruins, a faint hymn echoes through the building,
made from bodies and sounds of theories.

theories
beat their
chests in
the shape of
the sound
of machine
guns

Chile
They were out of bread.

Mutta
What will we eat?

Chile
There's only meal.

Mutta
Meal?

Chile
Yes, meal for porridge.

Mutta
Is that it?

STUTTER

Mutta
What's that shine in your eye?

Chile
I was stopped by one of the men.

Mutta
What kind of man?

Chile
A soldier.

Mutta
What did I tell you?

STUTTER

Mutta
Huh?

Chile
I don't know.

Mutta
What?

STUTTER

Mutta
What did your mother tell you?

Chile
That there ain't no more soldiers.

Mutta
That's right, baby.
That there ain't no more soldiers.

Chile
But–

Mutta
But nothing!
There are no more soldiers, okay. Okay?

STUTTER

Mutta
Say it.

Chile
There are no more soldiers.

Mutta
Again.

Chile
There are no more soldiers.

Mutta
I don't believe you child.

Chile
There are no more soldiers!

Mutta
Good good good. That's good baby.

Chile
But I saw the rifles.

Mutta
No, you didn't.

Chile
No. There were rifles with–

Mutta
You didn't see anyone with rifles. I'll tell you what you saw.
You only saw sticks.
People carry sticks, you know? You hear me?

STUTTER

Mutta

Cause there's just us that's left.
Persons. Humans. Folk, Mortals, Heads, Publics, Bodies-

Chile

You're doing it again.

Mutta

What?

Chile

Your words are catching.

STUTTER

Chile

One of the soldiers stopped me.

theories
surround
the mother
and the child
thrashing
theory
against
theory

STUTTER

Mutta turns her ears to the air, catching sound.

Chile

Then what was that?

Mutta's ears catch something else. Something from the air or the building.

Mutta

That's just them people making music.
You say one of the *persons* stopped you?

Chile

Yeah.
One of the *persons* stopped me.

Mutta

Baby, what did the person ask you?
Did you tell 'em you couldn't?
Did you tell them that you won't? Did you tell them you have a mother?
You don't talk to them like that, you hear?

Chile

Why not?
They're just *people*, right?

Mutta

Yes, just people.
If they stop you, *them.*
Tell them you have a mother, okay.
Okay?
Tell them you must take care of me. Tell them you don't know how to fight. Tell them you have carving hands.
Or washing hands, or mending hands.
But they don't understand, hmmm, do they?
Then you better make them understand.

Chile

They said if I go with them, outside the city. They said I can get paid money to help.

Mutta

Money. Money. Money.
What is it that they do when they go knock on doors in the night? What is it that they do when they go outside the city gates? What are you going to do with money?

Chile

More than the money, mother, they need me. Say they had been looking for someone like me. Said I have good eyes, and good hands. Say they could use eyes and hands like mine. Soft eyes. Sharp hands. Shiny eyes.

Mutta

I need you.
Baby, you think I don't need… You think I don't need you… You? You know that?

Chile

They want to be strong. Stronger than they are.
Said they need me so they can be stronger. I can be strong with them.

Mutta

And I don't want to be strong? Aren't I strong now?
Don't you do that.

STUTTER

Mutta

I said stop accusing me!

STUTTER

Chile

They said if I'm with them. That's one more, mother.
And things will be better if I fight with them.

Mutta

They have so many already. Can't you see there's just me?
I'm alone.

STUTTER

Mutta

They take take take take take take take take take–

Chile

Please, please, mother. It's okay.
It's okay–

Mutta

Them!
Amassing arms, buildings, children, minors, puppies
Everything!

Chile

You're doing it again.

Mutta

I know. I know.
I'm sorry. My words caught.

The mother attempts to embrace her child. The child evades his mother, but for a hand. The mother holds the hand of her child.

Chile

They need me.
They need my hands.
They only want my hands and my eyes.
You can have the rest of me.

Mutta

Sit down.

Chile sits on a pew just before the altar. Mutta comes behind Chile, hugs the child too tightly.

Mutta

What does help mean? Your soul for what?
My help. For what?
Not mine. They not getting.

The mother's hands grace her child's neck. Mutta's hands begin to close about Chile's neck. So tightly that she begins to strangle–

Chile

Let go. Let go. Mother!
Moth– Let me–
Let me go!

The mother's child gets away.

Chile

They never even stopped me. I followed them.
The soldiers. Soldiers. Soldiers. Soldiers.

theories take
the shape
of geese
and honk
the taunt

Soldiers. Soldier Soldiers.
I follow them every day to see what they're doing. One of them saw me looking.
He signaled for me to come. I almost went, but I ran.
One day.
I'm not gonna run.

The mother stutters before her child. Attempts words.
No words come.

Remember the world. Inviolate. World. Shreds. Species. Spin. Sung. Into existence.

Did you want to leave?

War horns. Fatalism excites. Taste. We sought. Never. Had no good. Answers. Instead. Filled.

War horns. Think. Predict. End against. Song. Sudden. Downward turn. Asks how. We live low. Refuse to. Low live.
This ode to kin. Apocalypse. Catastrophe.

When? Water. Consumed. The coastal. Peoples. Song. We thought. We thought. *We thought, this will teach everyone a lesson.* In theory. There. Deep. Measure. Of Time. Beats. Against our. Chests. Open there. No. Lessons in worlds. Ending.

NIGHT THREE | tear

Theory of Bessie arrange and sort the *Maize-Maize.* Theory of Bessie place the whole body of the plants onto the threshing floor.

Only when the theories have accounted for each stalk do they do the work of tearing and pulling ears from the dried stalks.

Some theories feed the dried stalks into the fire. Other theories listen to the fires hiss and crackle.

All the night Theory of Bessie tear and tear. When they have torn every ear from every stalk, the theories sing of love. The sound of love moves through the valley, up into the hills.

HOSPITAL

Noe
Where's your head these
days?

Wat
It sank in the river.

Noe
What took you so long?

Wat
The truck sank.
I doubled back.

Noe
I've been back for hours.

Wat
Someone followed me.
You prefer
I bring them here?

Noe
I prefer you to help me.
I prefer you to watch my
back.

Wat
That's
what I was doing. Did
you think I wasn't coming
back?

Noe
You weren't looking out.
You were just looking. I
signaled for you.
Nothing.

Wat
I was
looking out, and also
looking. I can do both.
Are you angry again?

Noe
We're a unit. You're not
focused. Did you see the
bridge?

Wat
Oh. I saw it. We should've waited until there were more trucks
on the bridge. I liked hearing the trucks crash into the water.
Did you see their arms flailing? They looked like they were
waving hello.

Noe
I signaled. Nothing from
you.

Wat
We've been separated
before.

Noe
Not for six hours.

Wat
Don't act like this.

Noe
I called your name.

Wat
That's stupid.

Noe
A sniper took a shot at me.

Wat
You can't run around
yelling names in the streets.

Noe
I panicked.

Wat
For a minute, it looked like
the trucks would float. They didn't.
They sank. They're made of metal.

Noe
Who was following you?

Wat
Can you put your hand

right here?
No, here.

Just like that.

theories
claw
hands into
stomachs

Noe
Did you hear me call your
name?

Wat
Good. That's good.

Noe
The bullet grazed my ear.

Wat
Did you bleed a lot?

Noe
Feel it.

Wat
You've had a lucky day. Do
you blame me?

Noe
I just want you to do what
you say you're going to do.

Wat
I heard someone yell
something. I couldn't make
out the sound.

Noe
I want you to say what you mean.

Wat

But I do.

Noe

You don't. Like that time you told me you were gonna help me explode the army base and make confetti of the general's brains in his own home so we could send all of them a message and you didn't even do that. We agree to a task. And then you do something else. We can't explode another bridge. We'll trap ourselves.

Wat

Take
your
hand off
me.

Noe

What?

STUTTER

Wat

What are you?

Noe

You weren't there. Anyone could've come from right behind.

Wat
I was looking behind.

Noe
Or from the side…

Wat
I had your flank covered.

Noe
Sure. And that would've been the end of me. Just like that. I gave the signal. I called your name. Nothing.

Wat
I could have been preoccupied.

Noe
I could have been killed.

Wat
I was preoccupied

Noe
What could have been so important? Nothing could have been that important.

Wat
I'm pregnant.

Noe
Don't be silly.

STUTTER

Wat
Say something.

Noe
Shit.

Wat
Something else.

Noe
How?

theories
echo
the how,
echo
a multitude
of hows

Wat
Something else.

Noe
Fuck.

Wat
Anything else.

Noe
Is it mine?

Wat
Do you want it?

Noe
Do you want me to?

STUTTER

Forget.

Men. Under rock. Grate teeth.
Against stone.
Take my hand!

Shelter your tremble.

Born. Third. Blue. Raise your hand. Feel the wind.
The blue third. Impossible. Reason corridor. Driven.
Sounded bodies. Blush. Speak.

You are.

Fleshly. Explode. Don't.

Burn with.

The head. What does the body show us?

Horizon.

NIGHT FOUR | shuck

Theory of Bessie, children of the long road, organize the *Maize-Maize.*

Theories shuck and cast silk and hull and ear after ear onto the threshing floor.

Holy thud after Holy thud.

STREET

Chile, Gucci, Wat, Noe and

Noe
Shhhh. Shhh.
It's okay.

GASP GASP
MOAN MOAN
CATCH

Wat
We had to beat the dogs away.

Chile
You're safe now.

Noe
Whatever you do, don't do that.

Chile
What?

Noe
Lie.

Gucci
There are no dogs here.

Kees attend a body in the street.

Noe

Nobody's safe in this street. And what are you doin' out
here anyway?

Wat

Don't you know you it's better to be indoors?

Kees

I've been on a
ground a like this.

Noe

This city doesn't like strangers.

Gucci

I thought it was a corpse.

Wat

Why are you out here?

Noe

It's not a corpse.

Chile

On the road to get food.

Noe

Why are you accusing him?

Wat

I'm not. I'm asking.

Kees

Lucky they didn't throw
them in the river.

Noe

They don't do that anymore.

Wat

That was years ago.

Chile

Can we get them off the ground?

Noe

And take them where? Home with you? And you, you shouldn't be touching them.

Kees

No one wants to be left like
this.

GASP GASP

MOAN MOAN
CATCH

Chile
What now?

Gucci
We get to work.

Noe
Water.

Kees
Help me pick them up.

Gucci
Is that rope?

Kees
I know a place.

Noe
Wait. We don't know if it's safe to pick them up.

Kees
It's fine. We have to
get them out of the
street.

Wat
Savages.

Chile
Water please.

Kees
No. Don't pour it.

Wat
Like this.

Gucci
Only savages would do that.

Kees
When you say savage…

Noe
More around the lips.

Wat
Open the mouth.

Kees
Have you ever been a
savage?

Chile
Wet.

Gucci
We have to get them off the street.

Chile
That's better.

Noe
Rise and fall.

Gucci
You haven't heard about the beasts.

Noe
Listen to the breath.

CATCH CATCH
MOAN

Wat
We shouldn't be out here.

Chile
Beautiful breath.

Kees
A friend went missing.

Gucci
Why can't we just leave them there?

Wat
Because we are not like them.

Noe
You think this could be your friend?

Kees
How can I tell?

Gucci
How tall was your friend?

Kees
About this tall.

Chile
Where can we take them? I want to help.

Wat
Not with us.

Gucci
I don't live in the city.

Noe
Fine. But let's get them off the street.

Chile
All the hair's gone. I have good hands.

Noe
It looks worse than it is.

Wat
Shoulders intact.

Gucci
Torso fine.

Noe
Feel the chest.

Chile
I'm touching the chest.
I can watch out if you need me to.

GASP GASP
MOAN MOAN
CATCH

Wat
It's all fine.
It's all going to be fine.
It looks worse than it is.

Chile
You're going to be okay.

Wat
Very good. You learn quick.

Noe
You don't know that.

Kees
You can't say that.

Gucci
That's what we say.

Noe
Relax.

Wat
You relax.

Gucci
We need more hands.

Kees
We'll need all the hands.

Gucci
Go and find help.

Noe
Why are you crying?

Wat
I don't know why.

Kees
I'll go. Stay. Attend the body.

Noe
More water.

Chile
There.

Gucci
That reservoir water?

Chile
We can't get to the river.

Gucci
The one they leave the bodies in?

Kees
Here, it's all we have.

Gucci
It's suddenly got so quiet.

Kees
Has it ever been this quiet?

Noe
You were looking for food all the way out here?

Theories honk and holler. Looking up. Gentle signs. Of departure. Skeins. Of black. Geese. Under sky. Black.

The migration. Of sound. Subject to object. Called. Out. To each. Others. Marking. Ways beneath. The cloud. Against lanes. Of sky. Belonging.

Bessie honks.

Sung solely. To the black. Certain of direction. Songs fall. From the sounded. Below others. Wings work.

Journey home. This we. Remembering. This we. Shaping. This we. Of the letter. Of the sound. The Shape. V. Shattering. Wings tired. With each. Death. Knells reform. The same lines. Of trajectory.

Wings rest.

To reform.

NIGHT FIVE | level

When the ears resemble a mountain, and there is no ear left to shuck, Theory of Bessie go about the work of leveling the *Maize-Maize.*

Hands sort ears on the threshing floor.

OUTSKIRTS

Gucci

How long we gotta stay out
here?

Loofa

You can't think up any new
question?

Ages

Until we can figure out what to do.

Gucci

Nobody even knows we're
out here.

Loofa

What'd you find today?

Gucci

Nobody knows we're out
here figuring.

Loofa

What did you find?

Ages

We know, we're figuring. Attention! Patience!

Loofa

Did you make it to the
library?

Gucci

What have I told you! There is no library!

Loofa

What used to be a library,
then. What did you get?
What did you find?

Gucci

Here. Take this. The good
it'll do.

Loofa exalts.

theories
pound
their chests,
drive
sound high
into the air

Gucci

Somebody exploded the
bridge.

Ages

Which bridge?

Loofa

Where'd you find it?
What was it with?
When's it from?

Ages

Which bridge?

Gucci

While we've been out here, what do you call it? *Listening*. For I don't know how long. People are vanishing. This is what I've seen: bodies are there

at night, and then those same bodies are gone in
the morning. I'm getting sick and tired of *listening*.
I'm getting tired of watching and waiting. The blue
bridge—it's gone.

Ages

It won't be long before there's nothing else in that city worth having.
The people will have to leave.
To give up on the fallen buildings, the meager rations.
You must listen. When they leave. We will show them where to go.
That is our work.

Gucci

Us? With what? These
scraps of paper. This music
he can't read. Show people!
Hah!
You haven't left this place
since we got out of the
university. I'm the one who
leaves. What are you gonna
show anybody? Who's
going to listen to you?

Loofa

I think this must be music.

Gucci

Tuh! What are you gonna
do with music?

Ages

If we don't attend to the territories of our spirit, then who will?

Loofa

It's our job to figure.

Gucci

As much as I like being outside. Outside the city. Outside of time. Outside my body, listening... Outside of the outside. I don't want to stay outside. People are siloed in the city. And you talk about these relics. These sounds you can't even read!

Loofa

Remember stew? That's
what I want.

Ages

You're tired. We all are.

Gucci

Do you hear what I'm saying?
Trapping all those people
inside the buildings.
They're cutting off all egress.
What are you doing?

STUTTER

Gucci

Stop doing that.
Will you stop!

Loofa

It is indeed a song.

Loofa belts discordant note
after note, each note uglier
and louder than the last.

Gucci snatches the paper.

Gucci

That's not what it says.
You can't know what it says.

Ages

Let him be. That's him. He does.
We wait and listen.

Loofa

And think. And imagine.
That's right. I do. You
complain. I never wait.

Gucci

Did you hear that?

theories
bark, croak
and
stridulate

Ages

Yes, wait. What is that?

Loofa

It's a cricket.

Gucci

That's not what a cricket sounds like.

Loofa

It's just some old dog.

Gucci

That ain't no dog. Lower your voice. Be quiet. It could be a soldier.

Loofa

But they're all dead.

Gucci

You think that because you sit out here, but they're not dead at all.

Ages

They're not dead.
They transformed.
We have to pay attention to the transformations.
The slight and the large.

STUTTER

Loofa

Meaning what?

Gucci

Meaning they worked for
the state. Meaning they don't
work for the state anymore.
Meaning they'll still take
your ear and put it your
asshole. They'll even pull
your teeth out. After that,
they'll wear your skin.

Loofa

Huh!
You can't scare me. You just
don't want me to go out with
you. Don't nobody want my
teeth.

Gucci

Teeth?
Teeth?
That's the least of
your worries.

Loofa

Stop trying to scare me.

Gucci

Oh.
The hordes invent things for teeth.
They invent things for skin.

Loofa

Like what?

Gucci

Don't they hate our skins? In the city, it's not just soldiers, there are the militias. The green militias. The gin militias. Oh and I almost forgot, the dog militias. Don't you know, there are packs of wild dogs that don't like you either. They've taken up residence in the hospital. In the hospital, they have a whole wing with just wild dogs. Some of them use our skins and try and put them onto their own.

STUTTER

Ages

The men who started this war do love the skin. They love to torture the skin. They also hate the skin. If you want to listen to something. Listen to this: when the skin has been tortured, the torturer longs for the skin untortured again. They want it fresh every time. Fresh skin is best. These long for the presence of the absence they've created.

Loofa

You think I care? Soldiers.
Mercenaries. Lamp militias!
Gin Militias. Dog Militias.
Come and get me.
I GOT TEETH! I GOT
SKIN! I GOT SO MANY
TEETH.
I GOT SO MUCH SKIN!

Gucci

Shut the fuck up!

theories
honk and
beat
their wings

Loofa

Oh, what are you scared?
Scared someone's come
and tie a rope around your
neck, hang you from a tree,
pickle your parts. Maybe
eat them!

Loofa collapses into a fit of laughter

Gucci

I said shut. The fuck. Up.
If you kill yourself out of
boredom, then fine. But
you won't take me with you.
I know about skin too. So
be careful.

*Recovering from laughter,
Loofa continues to sing and
make sense of the notes he
reads from the page.*

Gucci

I'm trying to tell you,
there's an industry around our
bodies. More and
more of them are
vanishing. Tell me, where
do the people go? Have you
seen any come down this
road? No. Then where are
they going? You don't see
what I see when I go into
the city. You sit here and
you, you– What is it that
you're even doing?

Loofa

I am archiving. I am an
archivist. This is important.

Gucci

Must be nice to have your scraps and build your little stories, oh excuse me---songs---with them. Tuh!

Loofa

I could go out, and you
could stay here for once.

Gucci

Shut up. You're not going anywhere.
You'd be dead so quick.

Loofa

How many years has the
war been going on?

Ages

I don't know. I've lost track. As long as I've been alive, and as long as my father was alive. Back when there was still a state.

Loofa

I thought it was a bunch of
states.

Gucci

No, the many states made
up the one.

Loofa

I can't help it. I don't
remember. You never talk
about your father. Is that
who taught you how to
listen?

Ages

So many cities were inside the great state. I don't know if there ever was one *state.* One and not one at the same time. Like you my father collected and preserved things, and like you he scorned listening. Now I have to agree. Some quiet. We've been up all night.

Loofa

See.
It stopped, anyway. Hah!
Told you it was just some
old animal.

Gucci

You don't know!

Ages

What if? There might have been someone as scared as we. And how do we act? How do we signal to them that we acknowledge their fear and our own? Again, before we sleep…What is virtue?

Gucci

Virtue is
(*performs sleight of hand*).

theories
wail

Loofa

Virtue is
(*performs making stew*).

theories
stomp

Gucci

Virtue is
(*performs levitation*).

theories
hoot

Loofa

No no no no no no no no
no. Virtue is
(*performs preservation*).

theories
hum

Gucci

No, virtue is
(*performs escapology*).

theories
cheer

Ages

Look at us. We're tired. We've been up all night. Now, there is dew. Virtue is dew on this blade of grass. See, listen to the blade quiver. When it quivers so, and the blade gets so heavy that it wants to crash of its own weight, but the dew is of such particular weight that the blade of grass does not spring, it only gets lower and lower to the ground, such that it releases the dew, and it slides off the blade of grass like a young child coming down a slide.

Gucci

That's all well and good when there's nothing to eat.

Loofa

Yeah, but what a beautiful
image.

Gucci

Is that image going to feed us?

Loofa

You know what?
Fuck you!

Gucci

Fuck you! And your images,
and your sounds, and your–

Loofa

Gucci's catching again.

Gucci

I'll calm down when you calm down.
Out of all the people. This is who I'm left with.

Loofa

What's a slide?

Ages

You are young.

Gucci

And foolish.
An old game. Everybody knows that.
An old instrument of play.

Loofa

From before?

Gucci

Of course, before. You haven't heard of one, have you?
You haven't seen any children sliding.
Have you?

Ages

Shhhhh. Listen.

Loofa puts his head down to
listen to the blade of grass.

theories
lower
themselves
to the
ground

Ages
Our words are like that.

Loofa
Like what, a slide?

Gucci
No, you moron.

Ages
Our words should perform that motion.

Loofa
Words slide?

Ages
Along your tongue, and into the earth to water it.

Gucci
Or to kill it.

Ages
Yes, or to kill it.
When the time is right.
we'll need the map you two are charting

The blueswoman stutters.
Into earth. She.
Dreams the earth.
Open. Swallow.
She whole.

NIGHT SIX | thresh

Theories emerge from the multitude bearing long cylindrical flailing sticks. Theory of Bessie beat the *Maize-Maize*, throwing their whole bodies into the effort.

A raucous sound vacates the throats of the multitude. Sounded bodies. All the night Theory of Bessie swing with their whole weight. The grain separates from the body, flies into the air, only to return to the threshing floor.

Twenty thousand breaths.

The work of separating kernel from ear, like the work of separating flesh from bodies, requires so many theories.

Theories to sort. Theories to sever. Theories to distort. Theories to consume. Theories to erase. Theories to forget the erasures.

The shape of dust.

Theory of Bessie thresh and heave and moan and grunt.

Those who do not thresh, feed the fire or echo the sound of the thresh and grunt all the night.

Twenty thousand breaths.

THE CHURCH

Mutta
You did it?

theories
hiss

Chile
Yes.

Mutta
How large is your debt?

Chile
A body debt.

Mutta
Why would you go and do that? With soldiers!

Chile
They're not soldiers.

Mutta
I should've never picked you up, but you had to open your mouth.

STUTTER

Mutta
Yes.
You made me hear you.
Do you know how I found you?

Chile
You never let me forget.

Mutta
That was a story you tell a child.

Chile
My mother left me with you.

A mother laughs at her child.

theories
cackle

Mutta
Hah!
I never told you this.
Listen.
I haven't told you about my work
Do you know there are stages to every war? There is the time when it creeps up, and lives in the words of persons, as they prepare to hurl their bodies, and all the extensions of their bodies: the metals, and tactics, and philosophies. All these to sever.
Sever time, sever shape, sever limbs.
When this war that has settled dust was at its apex, limbs lay out plain under the noon sun.
Hands, ear, lips. I collected every piece I could find.
Whole limbs, and later bone, and later bone fragments.
I can discern human bones from the bones of any creature, with just my eyes. I categorized, measured, indexed, tagged—with a whole team of peers who thought it important that we identify those who were severed.

And now when the war is waning, not because we are so tired,
but because there are so many less of us to kill,
even after there was no money to pay, and even after money no
longer meant anything, even after my colleagues vanished or
became limbs themselves, I kept working.
Each day at dawn, I walked the streets and picked up pieces of
mothers, soldiers, lovers, rebels, teachers, children…

theories
honk

I know the parts of every kind of person.
It was in one of these heaps that I found you.
You looked like someone's arm, and then you opened your
mouth.
Then you became
my work.

STUTTER

Chile
But--Now we'll be okay.
We won't be left in the streets.
I can get you bread.

Mutta
I don't care about bread.

theories
converge on
the mother
and child

Chile
I won't be a bad person. I won't do bad things.

Mutta
Get out!
Get out Get Out. Get out.

Get. Out.

theories
drag
the child
out of the
church into
the street

The body. Children eat.
The sun. Sound Bessie. Open. Her throat. A sky
taste. Blood written. Tritonal excitation.
Ruptured moons. Spoken oldly. Body violence.
Body hit. Body smack. Body lean. Body talk.
Body rock. Body peace.

Forget the night. Forget the noon. Forget the
second. Forget the chase. Forget the joy.

Forget to suffer.

Forget.
The killing.
Forget.
The air.
The fire.
The charge.
The excitation.
The crackle.
The body.

NIGHT SEVEN | regather

With hands, Theory of Bessie gather the kernels from the threshing floor, separating the hardened fruit from the silk and shuck.

Theories gather the kernels from the ground, shaking out the dust.

Theory of Bessie measure and weigh the weight of the *Maize-Maize.*

BRIDGE

Make's space is well put together. Witness Make with hammer and nail, measuring bits of scrap wood. Make pulls nails out of the wood, he repairs. He puts pieces of wood of various sizes together. The pieces are a little too weak to do what he needs them to do.

Kees Watches.

Make

Is there something you need?

Kees

You don't have
to stop on my
account.

Make

Is it something you want?

Kees

We were friends
once.

Make

Long time ago.
A lot's happened since then.

STUTTER

Kees

I need your help.

Make
What else is new?

Kees
There's a body
near the reservoir.

Make
There are bodies all over.

Kees
You found a body
once.

Make
I see bodies every time I go outside.

Kees
And you didn't
just leave my body
there.

Make
That was ages ago.

Kees
Not ages. Two
years, three
months, fourteen
days…
If we leave them
in the street. You
know what will
happen. I know
you know.

STUTTER

Make
You have some nerve coming back here.

Kees
This wasn't my
first stop. I walked
past this house
three times
before–

Make
And yet here we are.

Kees
Look. I'm not
saying you
owe me an
explanation.
You don't owe
me anything. If
anything, I owe
you.

Make
I don't owe you.
You don't owe me.

Kees
You know, there's
one thing I can't
wrap my head
around.

STUTTER

Kees

Clears throat. One
thing I can't wrap
my head around.

theories
clear their
throats

Make

God, what can't you wrap your nosey fuckin' head around?

STUTTER

Kees

A peace offering.

Kees offers a piece of fruit.

Make

What do you want?

theories
sigh

Kees

You can have it.

Make

It's fucking green.

Kees

You can give it
back if you don't
want it.

Make

Where'd you find it?

Kees

There's a tree, near
the bridge—

Make

This bridge?

Kees

The blue bridge.
The bridge
where you
found me.
The bridge we
can't get past.
The same bridge
the militias
won't let people
cross.

Make

I know the bridge.

Kees

The fruit doesn't
grow long before
they fall off but
it's a different taste
than the meal
porridge.

Make

Porridge is fine by me.
Bone is just fine by me.

Kees

You don't mean
that.

*Kees holds out the
fruit.*

Kees

Go ahead, take it.
Take it.

Make eats the fruit.

Make

Ahhh, that's good.
That's good.
That's good.

*theories
applaud*

Kees

Right?
Right?

Make

Yeah, God!

softens

It's been months since I saw you.
I thought maybe you were dead.
I forgot how lucky you are.

Kees

You know, the thing I can't wrap my ahead is how quickly we forget.

Make

What fool wants to go around remembering everything?

Kees

It wasn't so long ago…

Make

Tell me, what good is that?

Kees

That you found me. Body tore up, thrown over that bridge, like so many others. You helped me. You know the first body we found together? I saw him. He didn't recognize me, but I remember his voice. Something about the way he said hands. He said we need more hands. There's talk. You know the kind. Dangerous talk. We need a place. A safe place.

Make

Safe?

Kees

Safer. A safer place to bring
someone. We did this work
for years. You taught me.
Just this once, again. For
just a little while.

Make

I'm good over here.

Kees

Look I know
what you've gone through.

Make

You know what?

Kees

And I understand.
I know about your sister.

Make

Be careful.

Kees

I know you lost
your wife and
your child.
And your sister.

Make

You know about my people?

Kees

I didn't mean it
like that. I just
know you've lost
a lot.

STUTTER

Make

Lost? Lost?

Kees

Look.

Make

I don't need to look for nothing. It's right here.
Right fucking here.

theories
collapse
into
the earth

Kees

Where?

Make

Inside a row house. Before you get to this house, there is a street. With lots of what used to be houses. Used to be. The houses are done for. This house still stands. In it is a window. The slats hit the window when the air moves. The houses on this street are numbered. The houses on this street are bombed, torched, looted, razed. The number on this house is 621. We think: since there is so much loss here... Loss must be gone. Loss must have moved on. This will be a good place to rest. While we figure it out. The house is a row house. The row house next to it has a hole clean through it from what I believe is a tank. *A tank must have done that.* I find a good place to sleep on the ground floor near the window. The window is open. The air coming in is cool. It must be summer. I can't be sure if it is summer. I can hear the street outside. The seasons are funny. No tanks. No choppers. It is quiet. We are safe here. Upstairs. There is a good bed. Wife, Sister, Baby all sleep. Together. The baby holds tight on to a piece seersucker fabric we found on the highway. From the street, through the hole of the house, next door, you can see half a Queen Anne's couch. It is a very nice couch, except that half of it is missing. We think that if anyone does come, it will be in the night and not the day. We are having lunch. Good tins of salmon, and we have enough to last us a while. We are eating salmon with our fingers straight from the tins, while the baby is pointing to my forehead saying: *Borehead, Borehead.* Borehead. They ring the doorbell, and I answer. They kick me hard in my stomach. They take Wife and Sister upstairs. I hear their screams battle. All of the men follow. With the baby they smash her head into the table with one clean blow. They shoot me in the head. Then black.

STUTTER

Make

And then I wake up.
Want to know what I did after that?

STUTTER

Make

Ask me.

STUTTER

Make

Ask me.

Kees

What did you do?

Make

Ask again.

Kees

What did you–

Make

You're the dangerous one.

Kees

Can we bring
them here?
Please.

Say body. You heard. Bessie feeling against station. Against the plantation, against the narrow road. Against the limitations of resonance. Imagine pitch. Sound told.

What does a body say to us?
If I speak like this. Or
If I speak like this. Or
If I speak like – You imagine.
I sound. As you.
Imagine.

Bessie places her ear close to the earth to hear the earth. Do you know about the long road? That when we talked to our spirits that we didn't do it under the open sky?

That we did it in boxes black as night. Held the sky in the mind.

To recall.

What does a great-great-great-great-great great-great-great cousin look like? Do they look like you? Or you? Or you? Or you.

Do you know we are all wild with desire for something else?

NIGHT EIGHT | grind

Theories maneuver large stones onto the threshing floor.

Theories grind *Maize-Maize* against stone.

A high cry heard in successive waves across the valley.

Sounded.

Theory of Bessie dance *The High Alive*.

As the theories grind, their gestures become more pronounced.

Theories stretch within Theory of Bessie, shaking out from the past into the Living with moans, groans, shouts, and trembles.

Theories pour the ground *Maize-Maize* into the cast iron vessels.

BUNKER

Naif and
Rebl hunker down together. Tired from the work of gathering scarcity.

Naif
Were you shocked?

Rebl
Shocked?

Naif
By the blood.
When we were still in the prison,
before the red bridge fell.

Rebl
I was shocked at how little there was.

Naif
There was so much blood.

Rebl
Before the cell door opened.
I imagined there would be more.

Naif
The floors were caked with it.

Rebl
I thought the walls would be dripping in it.
I thought we'd have to wade through it.

Naif
You always hear about it.

Rebl
Did you get used to the screams?

Naif
No, never.

Naif picks up the sack. Casts the bones onto the floor before them.

Naif
Look our sacks nearly full. You think we have enough to trade?

Rebl
For a while.
We should never stop filling them.

Naif
I always do.

Rebl
Why you looking at me like that?

Naif
Tell the truth. You thought about me when you were locked up.

Rebl
I thought you were going to leave me there.

Naif
I started to.

Rebl
Then why didn't you?

Naif
I was scared.
I didn't want to walk out onto the road alone. Plus, you looked how you looked.

Rebl
You looked like–

Naif
Like what?

Rebl
You looked like an innocent.
And every one of those fucking guards....

Naif
They had all gone.
Left us in the cells to starve.

Rebl
Do you remember that siren?

Naif
And the ones they didn't hang or kill. They left us locked–
Which siren?
There were so many then.

Rebl
The first siren.

Naif
Of course.
They said they wanted the truth.

Rebl
They had us all in a line.

theories
fashion
sound into
alarm

Naif
They said information.

Rebl
They said they wanted the truth.

Naif
That's the first time I saw you. I saw you.

Rebl
Are we good here for the night?

Naif
They told the truth.

Rebl
I don't think I'll ever get used to that sound.

Naif
You're not supposed to.

Rebl
It's cold.

Naif
Come closer.

Rebl
It's getting colder.

Naif
Is that better?
We shouldn't have left them in the road like that.

Rebl
We have to look out for ourselves. Just you and me.
That's all we have right now.

Naif
You think we'll be safe again?

Rebl
We're safe right now. Don't you feel safe? Maybe if we get closer.

Naif

Then come closer. You can sleep.
I'll keep watch.

Rebl

Listen.
You hear that?
The dogs are close.

Naif

Shhhh.
I know exactly where they are.

Rebl leans into Naif.

Naif.

Keep quiet.
I'll listen.
You rest.

The body. As archive. Over. Heard dance. The body. As antiphonal. Texture. Of sounded matter. Made possible. Names. Before. The calling. The calling. Urges. Thought. Bessie. Adam. Michael. Francine.

The interred body. Pray seismically. Hurl. The body. In Space. Beyond. The untouched. Body infiltrates. Oblivion. The loud body. The Keisha body. Throws. Tina body. Spirals Levon's body. Totals. Revelation. Billions. Bodies. Severed.

The words of the song. The words of the body. The words of the song. The words of the body.

Bessie pulls the chord. With her.
Remember.

To listen.

NIGHT NINE | wash

Water spills onto the hands of the assembled masses.
You are of their number.

Theory of Bessie, maker of sound, invite you to eat.

Hold out your hand.

Theory of Bessie wash your hand. Water over flesh.

Theory of Bessie wash hands of kin and un-kin.

Theories wash the hands of theories.

TRIAGE

Noe
Did you go back?

Wat
I went.

Noe
Did they have bread this time?

Wat
No. The grain's exhausted. There's only meal.

Noe
Well, maybe next time.

Wat
Well,
I'm not going back again.

Noe

Why not?

Wat

'Cause after the grinders told me there wasn't any more bread. They told me to stop being sad.

Noe

Why?

Wat

Say it's best to forget about the baby.

Noe

What did you say?

Wat

I told them I can't.

Noe

You can't, or you don't want to?

Wat

What's the difference?
Hold on. Have you
been trying to forget?

STUTTER

Noe

So, you got mad again?

Wat

Answer me.

Noe

No, I'm doing the asking
this time.

Wat

Why won't you answer?
You should answer.
You have a way of always
asking.

Noe

Well.

Wat

Well, what?

Noe

Maybe there's a point to
leaving it behind.

Wat

Just like you…
I should've known.

Noe

You should've known what?
That maybe I want to leave
here and not spend my life
fighting militias? I do. So.
Did you get mad?

Wat

Now, you know I did. And
then, and then… They had
the nerve. *Them.*
They told me to stop being
mad. Wait a minute.
What did they tell *you* to
stop doing when *you* went?

STUTTER

Wat

Look at you.
And you did?

Noe
How mad did you get?

Wat
This mad.

Noe
How mad?

Wat
This mad.

Noe
Did you cut anyone this time?

Wat
Sure, I did. I always cut.

Noe
Did you see the blood once more?

Wat
I cut evenly… with all with my words. You would've been proud.

Noe
How did it feel?

Wat

It made me so happy. But my
sadness also made me happy.
I keep on telling you that the
people left in this city. Their
idea of happiness makes me sad.
Their ideas about happiness make
me sad which does not make
me happy. My sad makes sense
because it has sense. Even my
mad makes more sense than their
happy. They're getting sicker. You
should've seen him. There was no
bread left, and then he walked
out into the sun. He carried a
parasol so thick. A mask over
his face so thick, that I couldn't
make out his eyes. No one could.
There he was, speaking his sound,
through a barrier of cloth inches
thick. It muffled the sound.
Imagine!

Noe

That's no way to be. We can
try again.
We can be three if we try
again.

Wat

You don't look at me the
same anymore.

Noe

It's the same.
Maybe you forgot.

Wat

No, it's strange the way you
look sometimes.

Noe

What makes something
strange?

Wat

That it's not like us. You get
that?

Noe

We can try again.

theories
wail

Wat

The blue bridge is gone.

Noe

Did you have anything to
do with that?

Wat

There's only one way
out now.

Noe

Feel this.
Inside of here.
No.
Right here.
Here.

STUTTER

Did you journey far?
Did you forget the night?
Do you remember
the flatted fifth?
Agape. Torrents
of Not. Embed
the larynx. Species
of hold. Possibility.
Do you hold
light? Disappearing
war sounds
distinct. Opacity.
Morning and
Praise and
Sound. Anarchic.
Do you know what
feeds your people?

NIGHT TEN | serve

Theory of Bessie serve grits to the congregants.

THE FACTORY

BONE GRINDER

I smell the flesh. I singe the flesh.
My job is just a job.
Stop. Churn. Change. Break.

I smell the flesh. I singe the flesh.
I break the bone. I make the bread.

Singe the flesh. Smell the flesh.
Coarse spill. Speed trill.
Forty shins. Broken wheels.

I love the flesh

I smell the flesh. I singe the flesh.
My job is just a job.
Stop. Churn. Change. Break.

I smell the flesh. I singe the flesh.
I break the bone. I make the br–

Naif

Do you wonder about them?

BONE GRINDER

This is my job.

Naif

Some job.

BONE GRINDER

You're here aren't you.
Do you have something for me?

Rebl
Go ahead empty it out.

Chile empties the sack of bones out as
Bone Grinder weighs.

Naif
When you're breaking the bones, I mean.

BONE GRINDER
Hand over the sack or not. All the same to me.

Naif
When you're grinding the bones,

BONE GRINDER
I grind.
What else is there to say?

Naif
When you package the meal?

BONE GRINDER
I know that I'm doing my part.

Naif
When you trade the meal?

BONE GRINDER
What else would people do?

Naif
I know you know people know.

BONE GRINDER
I know it's best not to say that we all know.

Naif
Do you think they know?

BONE GRINDER
It's best if they don't know.
I put limits on the knowledge that I have.

Rebl
Let's make this quick.

THE BRIDGE

Kees
What's in the box?

Make
Air.

Kees
There's air out here.
There's air all around.
What's so special
about the air?

Make
I charged it.

theories
charge
the air

Kees
What are you
doing with the
air?

Make
I'm going to charge it with a dream.

Kees
But that box
kinda small.

STUTTER

Kees

I could get you
material for a
bigger box.

Make

Don't need a bigger one. My box is a good size.

Kees

I know where to
find shiny things.
I could get you
some. Just say the
word.

Make

Box don't need to be shiny.

Kees

Look out the
window.
Good.
Say, do you see
that dog?

Make

No, I don't see no dog.

Kees

That dog right
there.

Make

That ain't no dog.

Kees

You have to
squint.

Make

Nope. Nothing.

Kees

Squint you'll see
it. It's red.
Squint. Squint.

Make

Don't see no dog.

Kees

Must be a very
small dream then.

Make

What do you think?

Kees

I say there's a
red dog barking
there. Friendly
enough. Tail's just
a wagging. But if
there ain't no dog,
then okay.
Fine. Alright.
Well then, I say
can't no dream go
in a box.
Don't know no
kinda dream
belong in that
box. Won't fit.

So that box,
you're measuring
so carefully…
What's it really
for?

STUTTER

Make

You smarter than you look.

Kees

Been told that
before.

STUTTER

Make

Sure, you wanna know?

Kees

Yes, I'm sure.
It's what I've been
waiting for. I was
patient. I waited.

Of course, tell me.

STUTTER

Make

It's a suicide box.

Kees

Look. Come with
me. The city's
over. No one
can stay. That
reservoir. There's
no oxygen in it.
Thank you for
taking them in. I
came back for the
body.

Make

There is no body.

Kees

What do you
mean there is no
body?

Make

I woke, and it was gone.

Remember
the living.
Forget the war.
Remember
the signs of war.
Forget the sound.
Remember
the ten thousand two-hundred forty breaths.
Forget the monument.
Remember
the dead.
Forget the streets.
Remember
to forget.
Forget the
Forget.
Forget.
Forget.
For –

Theory of Bessie and congregants eat.

The body gets up. The body crawls down the street.

Body walks onto the street which is also a field, which is also then, which is also when and where you are.

Body leaves the city.

Body attempts sound.

Body utters the syllables Bah–Buh –Bah –Bah. Buh.

Body searches for sound.

Body sees the sound.

Body tries to catch the fugitive syllable.

Body catches and eats the Bah.

Once. Twice. Again. A fourth time.

Body lets the sound out again. Delights.

Body swirls through Theory of Bessie.

Theory of Bessie erupt into Sound.

Theory of Bessie echoes and envelopes. Body.

Body disappears into Theory of Bessie.

Body scatters the contents of the box.

Sound flies out from Body's mouth.

BODY

Wide.

Open.

Buh-own. BOOOOOOOOOOOONE. Buh-Own.

Scatter. Bone.

My throat.

Bone.

Choke.

GASP

Air. Bone.

Listen. Bone.

Bone.

MOAN

Air thinner, thinner. Thin. Thin. Thin.
thin thin thin thinnnnnnnnnnnn

Bone.

I, in my throat. I, in my mouth. No I. No I. No I.

Hand my hand.

Air high high bone.

Move. My throat.
Speech. Bone.

Bone Rock. Bone Time.

Bone Love. Love
Bone.

CATCH

Field bones. Bone fields.
Work Bone Fields Milk
Bone Fields Work Knuckle Bone. Bomb Bones.
Flood bone.
Iron. Bone. Milk bones.
Bone. Fields.

Bone fields.
Ground. Bone.
Knuckle Bone. Fist Bone.
Holler Bone. Bone Time. Time. Bone.
Holla

THE HIGH ALIVE | Body's sermon

Shout.
Welcome to the High Alive!
Shout. Shout.
The High Alive. The High High Alive. Alive Alive.

Alive.
Alive.
SHOUT.
Alive. High High. High High. High. High. Alive Alive Alive. Alive. Alive. Alive Alive Alive Alive Alive Alive Alive Alive.

Let the human fail. Let man fail. I say let the human being fail!

We have with us, for the first time in many long years, many long centuries...visitors, or better... Congregants!

Give our congregants a hand. Congregants give yourselves a hand.

Give it up for the visitor. I said give it up for our Congregants!

It was not long ago, that we sent out one from our own body, to take the gift and spirit of our people to another place. I want to ask you where is that place?

We didn't know the place...But what we decided that our bodies would remain our bodies. That I was done stealing my body. That no other living thing, only nature might take the breath which was sacred and a gift, and our inheritance, and that we would not be robbed of our inheritance, which is the issue of our ancestors.

What we demand of you, here, if you stay with us. Is that you kill yourselves. Kill yourself!

SUICIDE

Theory of Bessie prepare for suicide. Each theory within Theory of Bessie moves through the ritual space with the authority of their body. Of honk and holler and moan and excitation. In preparation.

Seventeen breaths. Theory upon theory shout The High Alive. Collapse and Restore.

Body tends the fire. The multitude regathers sound.

Eighty-six breaths. Wail: Well, well, well.

Theory of Bessie will body sound. Move forward as sounded body.

Thirty-Two breaths. Beat their chests. Rise and fall. Arms flail, fists clench. Bodies quake. Catch. Collapse.

Theories take on the horrors of these centuries past.

Twenty-Four breaths. Gentle
humming. Sporadic shrieks. Arms
flail. Feet stomp.

Theory of Bessie move through *passage* by their own authority. Listen. Hear their sound. Theory of Bessie spiral into sound.

Eleven thousand, five hundred twenty breaths. They braid silk and shuck, stalk, tassel, and root into their hair.

Ninety-six breaths. Theories. Gather hand with sound. Gasp for twenty-nine seconds.

On their heads. Braided Crowns.

Twenty-nine breaths. Spring up and down, while wailing. Tear clothes from body.

Body takes up the fire.

Five breaths. High keening. Shoulder shakes.

Theories, crowned in *Maize-Maize* bow, each one before the revenant body.

Forty-eight breaths. Running into the crowd. Tossed from one theory to the next.

Body, worker of fire, lights each braided sculpture. Hair, silk, shuck, stalk, tassel, and root.
Theories sing The High Alive.

Forty-Eight breaths. Collapsing into the ground. Fall and collapse.

Aflame, the multitude of theories shout. Theories not aflame move about the multitude attending the enraptured.

Seven breaths. Guttural Moans.

Theories burn or beat their heads with dust or burn their hands beating the flames.

Other theories do not burn, but take up and gather dust and witness or beat the flames out of existence.

Other theories feed the fire.

NIGHT | silence

Theory of Bessie and the congregation spend *Twenty-four thousand breaths* in Silence.

The lover rends the silence.

I am the lover

I want to stay with you in bed, draped in
white linen with cherry blossoms falling
through the window. See the trees blooming
in rapid succession? This light is thick, and
your fingers pay all the proper attention to my
back and inner thigh to my mons pubis to my
lips and when I bite down on your fingers you
keep riding, and I laugh, though I can't see
your face.

I am the mother

I stand inside the door where I stand
every dawn and look out onto a garden
phantomed by radiation. I breathe ash.
I eat ash. And shit this ash. And breathe
this ash. And eat this ash. And shit this
ash. And this ash and
and this ash, and this–
Sah. Sah.

I am the sage

One hundred years ago we leave the city.
One thousand years ago we leave the city.
Today we leave the city. We carry the
body. The body carries us. One breath
ago, we leave the city. We leave the city
between this breath and
the next.

I am the fool

I am brought from
across the deep sea.
The box in which I was
brought belonged to
pale conquerors who say
they love the world, and
rape and pillage every
place they touch. Raped
and pillage the world.
Hear me laughing?

I am the seeker

Into the dark, we go one by one, with not even the authority of our bodies, but the ability to think body, to sense body. We cry out. Hands press against hands. Body to Body. *Howl.* We howl. We howl in the belly. Howl years. Howl this death womb. Howl the dead and the living high singing the high even in the dark in the deep of the box on the water.

I am the child

Outside of the city, I move against the mother. The mother wants to hold me. I am the child who leaves the mother. See how I run. I run far so that I can long for the mother. When I am my mother's child, I cannot run.

I am the outlaw

Our soul leaves our body. We travel as war takes shape. We hear the before. We watch The Civil War, and Hiroshima and when you listen you hear Biafra and The First and Second Congo Wars, and The Football War, The First World War, The Vietnam War, and the war we don't have to dream, the war we know in our bones, The War that Settled Dust. In our dreams, we fight on every side.

I am the creator

When the soldiers come to the house,
they stand in front of your father's
father's father's house, gazing. Your
father's, father's, father's father gives
them water. They ring your father's
doorbell. Inside, your father's father's,
father's, father smiles. Your father smiles,
invites them in.

I am the magician

Forget time.

I am the innocent

Remember to leave the city. Remember
to run if you need to. Remember the
dawn, and stew, and buildings if you
want to, and keep record. Remember
shape. Remember to forget your shape.
Remember the hills wet with dew.
Remember the hills wet with blood.
Remember the morning.

I am the lover's lover

Are you still there?

THEORY OF BESSIE

Kill the myth.

Do you have enough love?

Is your body

When all you can do is stutter.

You can do better than that.

Do you know you've been seen?

Do you know?

enough?

Is your mind enough?

When disaster rings your doorbell.

Shout for the one who left and will never return.

You can.

Theory of Bessie ululate.

Then it gets so quiet, that you can barely hear the…

Body chants. Theory of Bessie join.

Body disappears into the multitude.

We are the Body. When we are not the Body. We tear skin off
cities. We silence. We open chests. We silence. We look inside.
We take bone. We look inside. We look inside we. We see
ourselves. We theory we.

We theory we theory we theory We
theory. We theory We theory we. we Theory we.
we Theory we. we theory we. we theory we. we Theory.
We theory We. We theory We. we theory. We theory we. we
theory we. we theory we. We theory we. We Theory. we
Theory. we Theory.

So Quiet. So still.

Charge the Silence.

Rend the Silence.

NIGHT | ephemere

Theory of Bessie turn away—makers of signs or children of the moon or fools of infinitude or multitude of the stutter or shouters of the alive or moaners of the tritone or sounders of shape or gatherers of fire or severers of flesh, body of sound and shape—turn away from you, regather their sounded bodies and return.

They leave for you the empty vessels. They leave for you the ash and the rent silence.

They leave for you the fragment.

Each theory within Theory of Bessie leaves for you, the foot print in earth, the echo of song, the cast iron, the unsettled dust.

Theory of Bessie leave for you –

Loofa

It's been too long. I miss
him.

Ages

Brother tell me, what is home?

Loofa

What if he's not coming
back?

Ages

Brother tell me where does the past begin?

Loofa

You should've sent me
instead.

Ages

At the point when one road ends another
begins.

STUTTER

Loofa

How do you know if you're
dead?

Ages

We are alive.

Loofa
Prove it.

Ages
Feel this.

Loofa
That don't mean nothing.

Ages
Feel it.

Loofa
That doesn't prove
anything.

Ages
It's not something you can prove. It's something
you have to know. It's a decision you have to
make. Listen.
I'll listen with you.

Theory of Bessie sing the discordant tone to the night wanting proof.

Ages
Do you hear that?

Loofa
No, I don't hear a thing.

Ages
Listen again.

Ages

Listen like this.

Loofa and Ages listen.
As the listening intensifies.
Theory of Bessie lift the discordant tone in praise of the living.
Gucci, returns.

Gucci

The bridge is gone,
If we're going to leave, it has to be now. We have to be careful.
Herds of wild men are waiting to do unspeakable things.
Agents of the former state.

Ages

Slow down. Slow down.

Gucci

We have to go. Now! The people are gathering on the road making their way out of the city. Not just a few of them, but all of them. We said we'd help when it was time. It's time. Let's go. What's he doing?

Ages

Listening.

Gucci

To what?

Ages
To his *alive.*

Gucci
That's great but we gotta go. We have to go now.

Theory of Bessie, after much tarrying, journey back into the hills. Leaving their sound behind their body.

Ages
And so we'll go. What is virtue?

Gucci
We don't have time for that. Are you crying?

Loofa
I think so.

Gucci
Why are you crying?

Loofa
I heard my alive.
Do you hear yours?

THE HIGH ALIVE

AN EPIC HOODOO DIPTYCH

THE LIGHT BODY

Land Acknowledgment

The 3rd Thing is located at the southern tip of the Salish Sea on the unceded land of the Medicine Creek Treaty Tribes: the Nisqually, Puyallup, Steilacoom, Squaxin, S'Homamish, Stehchass, T'Peeksin, Squi-aitl and the Sa-heh-wamish. As part of our work to create a culture of intimacy, accountability and radical imagination, we acknowledge the violent legacy of settlement and ongoing colonialism and commit to cultivating restorative relationships with Indigenous communities and with the land.

In support of truth-telling and reconciliation, and with the belief that a book can be a liberated and liberatory space that travels through time and across borders, each of our 2020 Cohort authors shares their pages with Melissa Bennett, an Indigenous writer whose work serves as an invitation to listen more closely and to more voices.

Melissa Bennett

Melissa Bennett, M.Div. (Umatilla/Nez Perce/Sac & Fox/Anishinaabe) is a writer, storyteller, story listener, educator, and spiritual care provider living as a guest on Medicine Creek Treaty Tribes land. Melissa is interested in story as medicine, especially its ability to heal historical trauma among Indigenous communities. The series of poems printed at the front of The 3rd Thing's 2020 titles is meant to reflect the ways in which our lives are intertwined with the stories and memories of our ancestors and our descendants. They bring the past, present, and future together through place, people, traditions, culture, and faith practices. These poems ask where we have been and where we belong as the story of our own becoming.

Belle Passi & Blue Mountains

by Melissa Bennett

I am from "she gave you up because she loved you"
and "you know your grandmother was a patient there"

I come from between depression glass candy dishes
and painted parfleche, grandma's suitcase

From in between chasing ponies, keep the one you catch
and Ouija board nights channeling Jim Morrison until morning

I am from carrot cake shaped like rabbits
Saturday night hamburgers and double chins

I am from the red stain on your head when you died
blood pooling at your hairline

I come from between snakes poking their heads from the Deschutes
and fifteen bears dancing in the night, rubbing against human legs, singing

From the pedophile who looked like a surfer lost in the desert
and the braids my grandmother kept to transform her 1920s bob into Sacajawea

I come from between bloated cows on grassy hillsides
and thunderbirds with hailstones dotting an orange landscape purple

I am from angels in stained glass, wings covering their faces
and Quinalt strawberries in shallow ground

I come from the center of church attics like sacred caves
and ancestors in galaxies of cedar steam

I am made of onions and Marion berries, cow tongue, and suckin' candy
I am nusux and corn husk bags, red beaded roses, and prophetic preachers

I am from the woman who killed a confederate soldier with a shovel
and the grandfather of the man who became the greatest athlete of all time

I am generations of dead in Blue Mountains
and graves beside onion fields in Belle Passi

The 3rd Thing

editors@the3rdthing.press

Bookseller & academic distribution
is handled by Small Press Distribution, spdbooks.org.
Support the press and writer with your individual purchases
through the3rdthing.press.

Cover & book design by Anne de Marcken
Cover image, Juan Alonso-Rodríguez

Typeset in Garamond, Century Gothic and Origin Super Condensed

Printed in the United States of America by
Spencer Printing.

ISBN: 978-1-7344071-2-9

LCCN: 2020931511

FIRST EDITION

THE HIGH ALIVE
AN EPIC HOODOO DIPTYCH
THE LIGHT BODY

Carlos Sirah

The 3rd Thing, Olympia, Washington

for Samuel

I love the Lord
He heard my cry, and pitied every groan.
Long as I live, while trouble rise,
I hasten to His throne.
Traditional Metered Hymn

Baby, won't you shave 'em dry?
Want you to grind me baby
Grind me 'til I cry.
Lucille Bogan

I'ma go outer space one time, just one time
I'ma go outer space one time, just one time
Watch me
Watch me
Big K.R.I.T.

When your leg was still your leg
and not a ghost leg
you walked each row
made
sure each seed breached
Dancing flames ring the cotton field
I dip and arch while you push the tractor
So we courted over three bitter seasons
Then in a copse of dense cool fern
vexed
only
by deer
I kneel
a wooden flute
you mount
a knife in clay.
You always laughed being insecure.
Averting my gaze
you peered up through the trees.
Called to a thousand times
You never looked back.

Where autumn crosses the desert and the field crosses the temple and the wood crosses home and spring crosses wilderness –

Capture Release Dig Hold

–SHU–
enters
the worlds.

AUTUMN

Tallahatchie

In the front room, Noah stands naked before the mirror. Beside Noah. A table. On the table. A Straightedge. Corner. A bar of soap. Center. A basin. Next to the basin. One of those funny little brushes for lather. Nearest Noah. A carafe of water. Folded primly. A white towel. Attached and hanging from the table. A leather whetting strop.

In the front room, there is also a window, which looks out onto the land. Rows and rows and rows extend until they reach a wood in the west where each day the sun sets over hard pine and red oak and sweetgum.

Noah

Micah

Noah

Gaze

Noah

Silence

You gon' clean that mirror?

I know my face, Micah.

Do you want to get cut again?

Veteran of these Forever Wars
Noah the Amputee
pours water into the basin.

You gon' cut yourself if you don't
clean that mirror off.

Mane, go back to bed.

You're up.
I can't sleep.

I been living with the same face for
25 years Micah.

Micah
Keeper of Bees
Lover to Noah
gazes at his Love.

I think I got a really excellent handle on what
my face look like right now.

Do you?

Matter of fact, I do Micah.

Did it happen again?

–SHU– watches you watch.

Silence

Is something happening?

I got this.

All I'm saying is that you owe it to me
to let me know if anything is happening
that I might need to be aware of.

Owe you. Owe you?
Nigga what I owe you?

Your debt's not forgiven.

Did you see something?

Hear something?

Gaze

Why you up at me at three o'clock in the morning talking bout-

Noah, are you hearing things?

-I owe you something?

Micah gazes.

Mane…
You better take your narrow ass back to bed.

Micah gazes at-

What do you want!

Silence

You sometimes use it as an excuse.

It?

The mirror.
Or the field, Noah.

Noah picks up the soap.

Excuses to not talk-

Noah drops the soap into the water.

-about what's actually happening
with you. With us.

Man, I'm just shaving.

What are you doing staring into that mirror?

Noah tries to make-

At three o'clock in the morning-

-lather with the soap.

-you're in here shaving?

Bae-

You-

-I don't understand why you can't

-been fucking with my soap again?

-just talk to me.

Gaze

And put some clothes on.
It's cold.

Found on Ebay. Adedayo's African Market.
Look how we use each other.
Why do we meet where the blade cuts?
Walk the thin line between this world and the other.

Somebody moved my fuckin' soap.

Remember when we used to talk Noah?

I done told you about moving my shit around.

Micah gazes.

You know I need things to be where they are.

I would ask you things.

I need my things to stay my things.

Remember when you would answer me.

Noah tries harder to make lather.

Babe, you could out-talk me.

Noah puts all his will into making the lather.

About nothing sometimes.

The soap in the basin will not -

We can talk about nothing

-yield to his will
nothing will.

Nothing can be something sometimes.

Noah stands before yet another failure.

We'd talk.
For hours and hours and-

It is three o'clock in the morning.

-and hours Noah.

Please leave me alone.

Remember, Noah?

Silence

I want to be alone.

Silence

Micah gazes at his Love.

Noah's eyes,
pools of dark.

I live with you.

I just want to get up.

You're up.

I want to shave my face.

How sharp is your blade?

You're shaving Noah.

I want to do it alone.

Micah gazes.

This morning?

Noah.

Can I have it?

Sure.
You can have it.
Take the day.

Gaze

Mane, I swear ‘fore God, Noah
if you didn’t talk in your sleep
I wouldn’t know shit.

What?

Since you stopped talking to me
I have to get that glass
put it to your chest
see if your heart’s still beating.
At least you talk in your sleep.

What are you talking about?

Dogs.
Shadows.
Deserts.

Since when?

Since we couldn’t stay in the city Noah.

Noah gazes.

Since we ran. Back to this fucking town.
Shit this ain’t even a goddamned town.
These fields. The dust on everything.
Since you been getting up every morning
before day, staring into that mirror.
Since you only have time for plows and tractors
and fields and-

We didn’t run.

We left.

No nigga, we ran-

We just left.

-in the middle of the night.
Like runaway slaves.

You didn't have to come.

What the fuck you just fix your mouth to say to me?

Are you real?
Prove it.

Silence

Whom did you last cut?

Taken from the bark of a hard pine in the wood beyond the field.
Hollow, can you hear me? Can you hear me, hollow?
Always better at climbing than you. I climb. You fall. Our way.
I speak to your hollow. Give it a home. Close to me.

You said we gon' work together to build something.

Noah picks up the blade.

So I get in the car with you.

And drive in the black of night.

-and every time I look up you out in the field.

You in the field plowing.

Nigga, don't point that fuckin' blade at me!

Noah tests the blade against his finger.

Noah begins whetting the blade.

With you talking shadows and holes and-

Whetting.

Noah gets lost in the whetting.

Lost in the reflection of his blade.

What?

Look at me Noah.

Taken from Noah's lunch sack.

Who saves half of peach?

When we are ten. We let the fruit rot. Dry the pits beneath the sun. With a host of cousins, we wage a child war across fields and into the wood. Noah on one side. Me on the other. The Pit Wars.

Recall the flesh. Nectar on skin.

DISPATCH

front door

Dear Noah,

You are so paranoid! You say the light flickers outside
the house every time you get home from the field. So,
you come home and put on that same Art Ensemble of
Chicago album to calm your nerves. It's free jazz Noah. It's
ain't not supposed to calm you down. What kind of brain
do you have that jazz calms you down?

Noah, I know when you look in the mirror, you
don't see yourself. Not because you are no longer there.
Your leg was the first to go, but now I'm having
trouble finding other parts of you. I know the glass
that we found in the field is not yours.

Fuck!

Did you stay over there? Who's watching us? What people?
I don't want you to disappear. ~~But you~~ No. We
are in danger. If you can pretty please.. Go back
to Iraq and find your fucking leg.

Yours,

Micah

WILDERNESS

temple

This wilderness.

A temple asks Noah
What about the wilderness?

It's different here.

A temple invites Noah to recount.
Go back.

7
6
5
4
3

2

A temple always says
Begin.

And then I fall.
I fall as
through an eddy
where the world
I know is no longer
and the desert
invites me
to behold.

A temple stops time.
Where does the eddy take you?

Into the pit.

A temple blinds.
Who's in the pit?

The wolf.

A temple travels.
Do you know the wolf?

No, but the wolf knows me.

A temple dwells.
When did you first meet the wolf?

Now, it's not a wolf. It's an osprey.

A temple opens its doors.
I'd like to put the question to you again. What is love?

The negotiation between this world and the one beside it.

A temple holds high the song.

You say there is another world, and it is inside this one?

All I know is that I'm falling
falling down the snake hole
falling into the eddy
falling up into the sky
falling sideways into winter.

A temple destroys time.
What do you see when the osprey looks at you?

I can't see it.
I look through him.

A temple praises opacity.
Is it your lover you look through?

It is not my lover.
It is a shadow.

A temple sits in repose.
Is it a shadow that you've seen before?

It is the shadow of the sun.

A temple laughs.
Do you think you're the sun?

I am a body on earth.

A temple colors its walls orange in consideration of that day.
What about your missing leg, Noah?

My leg is inside my mind
which is inside the space
which is your mind
which is also a dark cave
which is also the salivating dogs
that we shoot
on the side of the mountain
every time.

A temple recoils,
Did you ask to shoot?

I told you I asked.

looks Noah in the eyes,
Why did you ask to shoot Noah?

We had taken care of the animals for so long.

then beckons.
Why did you ask Noah?

I dream about killing all the dogs in the world.

A temple weighs.
Why did you ask to ask to shoot?

I didn't want to shoot.

A temple becomes a doctor.
Good. And now?

This terror.
No sleep.

A temple would prescribe.

We can fix sleep.
Paxil.

I wretch.

A temple would be medicine.

Wellbutrin?

I sleepwalk.

A temple sees the hole.

What about Xanax?

I eat it all.
To take the place of the loneliness.
To fill the space of the loneliness.

A temple desires knowledge.

Does it fill the space?

I can no longer see the space as clearly.

A temple holds encounter.

So, can you move in the space of the loneliness?

I wade through it.
It's like thick hot cream.

A temple remembers the refrain.

Do you still have your leg?

Sometimes I am whole being.

A temple makes possible the chorus.

Can you see Micah in this space which you call loneliness?

Micah says I have a take monster.

A temple laughs at Time.

Did you say take monster?

Micah says I steal time
that I steal his heart.
That our hearts are clocks
that can be stolen.

A temple mocks.
And what do you believe?

My take monster takes from me.

A temple fishes in the desert.
What does your take monster take from you?

It takes heaviness and gives me back hollow.

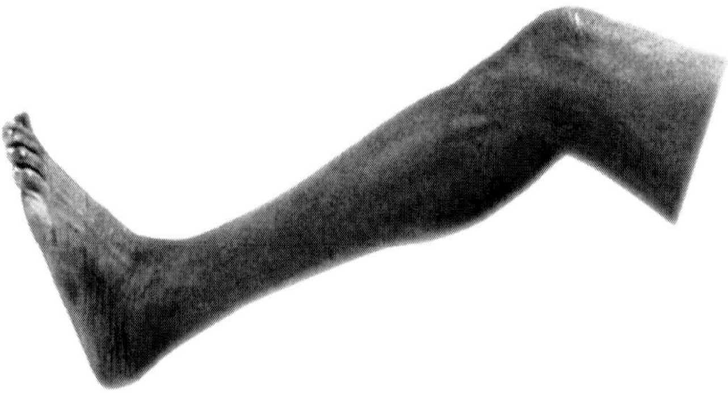

A temple presses against the body.

And what about your blade, Noah?

It's sharp. It feels good on my skin.
It cuts like a good blade should.

A temple shadows the soul.

Is that all?

When I press it to my skin, even a little it bleeds.

A temple extols sacrifice.

And what about the blood?

Sometimes I want to see the blood grow into a big pool around my head.

A temple fashions discourse.

And does the blade produce pain?

Not a real pain.
A shadow pain.
Ache is a better word.

A temple carries the body.

Can you describe the ache?

Ache like a trumpet.
Like the sound of a trumpet with blankets over it.
There is another world, and I am inside of it.

A temple thirsts for adoration.

Why did you start shaving your whole body?

To get clean.

A temple keens the air,

When you fantasize do you think it'll happen with your blade?

Rather a word which is a blade.

hones the blade,

Do you want to cut Micah?

I don't want to cut Micah.

reappoints the spirit.

Do you remember the words?

Carry me into the sun.

A temple recalls Noah's gods.

Last time you said...

Oh. Yes.

Carry me behind the sun.

SPRING

Micah dances the Hi Holy Ha

When spring silences
wilderness and the woods
silence home and autumn
silences the temple and the
field silences the desert-

–SHU–
unsettles
the worlds.

I turn my ear to the woods. Between the trees,
my lover's image.
Hi Holy Ha
Between the folds of time, I gather
within the wood
beyond the field a
Ha
Holy feet on the hot soil of my earth with my lover's heart. I,
holding his Him in my arms.
Holy Ha How? *Ha* How did I? How *Hi* did I hoist my love upon
my back? His eyes rolling into the back of his head. Hot foam on
his lips. *Ha* my love grunts and heaves. *Ha* I carry my love, head
bouncing on my shoulder. Body quaking. My lover's body. *Ha*
Ha Ha
Hi Hi Ha
Ha My mind.
Ha Didn't give.
Ha We. *Ha* Song.
Sing *Ha*
Ha Ha
Beyond the rows
the wood.
Hi
Holy Ha
Ha Ha
Hi

Between fights, we watch a war documentary. I read Noah's face
for any sign. Rust. Erosion. Scales. He yields nothing. I get so
tired.
Goodnight, I tell him.
The following night we read a poem.
I read one line.
Noah takes the next.
This line about teeth and indentation stops him.
Noah weeps.
Ha The night.
Look at me, I tell him.
I am here.
He will not cross
to me. *Hi*
The night after, I get him to dance. He looks happy. I brought
him oranges from the market. *Hi* He places one of the oranges
on the center of the table. He rolls it from one end to another.
He won't stop.
He invites me to play the game. He gets like this. Tonight, I
resist. I don't appreciate the monotony of his landscapes. It's like
Noah to create another distance between us.
Noah says it's my fault.
How? *Ha*
Noah says the earth opens, or the table splits, or his mind severs
from his mind. I can't see the cracks
he claims to see.
Holy
I am only an expert in his physical being. That is what I measure.
I want him to remember the splits in our bodies. Where his arm
folds. The *Holy Ha* between his thighs.
the split of his ass.
Where my mouth opens and utters a
Hi Holy Ha

In the unheaven of the hospital that night, I hovered in the corner beneath a shape I hadn't seen in forever, not since my dog,
Zeke drowned in Lake Enid.
While treading water, I, Zeke and a boy whose name I can no longer dance, dove down to save my dog.
Only I made it out alive.
Hi Holy Hi
That night, Noah slept at the foot of my bed.
Tonight, I sleep at the foot of his.
I call upon Aunt Harriet, my grandmother' sister who visits me in dreams, carrying Zeke in her arms.
Mothers in Heaven. Guide me tonight!
This man, a blade in my side will kill me!
Will make me unfit for love again!
In my dreams, we sit at the dinner table.
It is Thanksgiving.
We feast.
Inside the dream, at our table, we speech gratitude.
Of gestation. Of harvest. Of bounty.
Noah's father returns from the kitchen with libations. Seagram's Seven. He pours for the living and the dead.
It is only when we have raised our glasses, swallowed the sloe-bitter drink, registered the space between, only then do I recognize Noah's leg on the table.
His father carves the leg meat
into thick even slices.
We feast and laugh.
Noah's eyes, pools of dark.
His mouth, a cavern.
Tonight, in the hospital
I turn my ear to your chest again.
When I listen closely, I hear a
Ha

AUTUMN

beaver killing

The Scorpion?

Yeah, Micah. The red one.

It was orange.

The one with the Shimano SX pedals.

Yeah, nigga, the orange one.

You thinkin' about the tricycle.

Noah, a tricycle is not a bicycle.
Besides, the tricycle wasn't yours.

There you go.

It was your brother's.

Who gave it to me.

She told you don't let them ride it.

Who?

Who? Your mother.

No, *who* she say don't let ride it?

She said very specifically, Do not. Let those…

What?

Look I ain't gone say what she said because I'm like a for real Christian.

Okay.

But she was very specific about who was not to ride the bicycle. And what do you go and do?

Noah gazes.

Huh?

Let my cousins ride.

You let those *so and so's* ride it. Your mother was right. She was a prophet. A false one, but a prophet.

Don't talk about my mother.

Micah gazes.

Yeah, and they broke it.

What about the *orange* bike?

Did you ever ride the Scorpion?

Didn't need your bike. Blue. Raleigh. 10-speed. Adult.

You could barely get on it.

I still have it. Still blue. That's the kind of man I am.
You know why Noah? Cause I didn't let my cousins ride it.

You didn't have any cousins, Micah.

Fuck you. Where your bike at?

Why do you always do that?
Oh my God. You were really upset.
So jealous. I had speed.

Jealous. Never.
Confused. Maybe.
You could barely ride it.

Your black ass was jealous.
And we were 11

How do you remember that?

That's when I got my rifle and it didn't snow.
It rained ice and when the ice landed on the all
the trees, it froze. The ice froze solid around the
branches, even the leaves. We woke to the sound
of trees splitting. Cracking. Do you remember?
We were 11, because they said, *that's when you get
a rifle*. Not 10, but 11. This is when our pipes
froze. We had to go the artesian well to fill all
the buckets, even the tall rubber trash cans. We
filled them all with water. Daddy was up under
the house building a fire to burn away the ice,
to free the pipes. The pipes had expanded so
much. So they burst. The power lines split in
two. Remember, we couldn't play Zelda? So
I turned my gaze to the field. The birds had
come to drink the water from a pool in the field.
Mostly blackbirds. All morning, I shoot mostly
into the air. In between the shots, tree limbs
heavy with the weight of the ice crash to the
ground. Among those birds, there is another
bird, a red one. I can barely see it. Noah,
how could you forget the sound of the trees
cracking? When the birds take flight. Into the
flock, I aim and fire and miss. *Take your time.* I
hear my father's voice in my head. *Breathe.* I tell
myself. So I take my time. I breathe. When I see
the cardinal take flight, I am the stillest I've ever
been. I watch the red through the rifle's sight.
Between one breath and the next, I squeeze the
trigger. The blackbirds scatter. The cardinal falls
into the pools Giddy with accomplishment. I
laugh. That's the first and last time I ever killed
anything. Intentionally.

You were bored, what'd you expect?

Micah gazes.

Didn't you kill a six-point buck that next fall?

My dad lied.
Wanted a man.
Said I killed it.
I had the shot.
I didn't want to.
I refused.

We could go again now.

Silence

I'm sorry.
I didn't mean that.

I don't know what's wrong with me.

Gaze

The bike, Noah?

Was that before Nita died?

Yes. Before.

Before you were baptized?

No, I got baptized the following summer.
The revival my cousin came from Detroit.

Oh my god. With the car!

With the car we stole.

Nigga! With the talking car we stole!

She told us we could sit in it.
She didn't say drive.
You always like to test.

You wanted to be Michael Knight.

Noah sounds the Knight Rider theme song.

I thought, Man, who is this woman?

But she wasn't a woman was she?

She was. She had children.

What was her name?

And a husband. They called her Nectar.

Your uncle kept on calling her Arthur.
I thought that was weird.

And we called her Nectar.

Nita was like, *They take the flesh, the penis flesh* she called it.
They slice it in half, and then they make a pussy out of it
Just like that.

My mama told your mama that she had both.

They made her choose?

Her parents chose.
She was Arthur while they grew up
and when she came back
she was Nectar.

She had like six kids.

All adopted.

Oh yeah, she had a husband.
She brought him to church.

If she built a family
out of nothing
so can we.

She saved that house, didn't she?

Did you really want this house?

Gaze

We raced. I was on my red Scorpion.
You were on your 10-speed. Major.
and Nita. Major's bike didn't have any
brakes. He crashed at Earl's bus stop.

That crazy nigga.

With his bathtub out in front of his bus.
Nigga living in a bus.

Did he ever try and get you on his bus?

Never.

Never?

Okay, yeah, but I never got on.
It was on the way to the creek.

We raced.
All the way to the creek.
Where you killed the beaver with your knife.

The creek that separates us from the peckerwoods.

You busted that beaver up side its head.

Why'd you look away?

'Cause I didn't want to see you do that.

I kept thinking about them slicing my dick.
And why would she want somebody to do that.

So she could be her.

Was that the summer you stopped going to church?

You didn't have to kill it.

I needed to see what it looked like.

to slice the flesh.

That shit that's haunting you.
It ain't me.

You really think we could
make a family?

DISPATCH

nightstand

Micah,

Stop leaving these dumb notes on the fucking refrigerator. If you want to say something real to me... SAY IT TO MY FACE!

So I can snatch the larynx out of your throat with your smart ass mouth. Please avoid me when I come home from the field tonight and go fuck with your bees or something.

Matter of fact, why don't you sleep out there by that apiary, 'cause you obviously care way more for them bees than you do for me.

Your Servant,

Noah

P.S. The light does flicker.
I'm not imagining things.

AUTUMN

life's games

Found in Noah's field, entangled in cotton root.

I wanted to leave this bottle there in the ground.

You brewed mushroom tea, poured it in the bottle. We drank. Said you saw gods in the fields. I drank. No gods came for me.

I call every spirit who drank from this bottle. To witness. I call every ghost of these field. To witness.

Was he dead or was he alive when you entered the room?

Micah.
Man, what you doing?

Was he?

I don't know.

Was he dead or alive?

I don't know.
I told you. Babe.
I can't remember.
Wait-

Was he dead?

Babe. Look at me.

Micah gazes not at Noah, but at the space between them.

There's a limit to how much
I can take. I will take. How much
of this I will sit here and keep taking from you without any real
way to figure out-

Figure out what Noah?

What's real, Micah.

Found beneath our bed.
I don't trust him with shit like this.
I watched you watch your mother on the horse, with the lariat, roping the calf.
I use you to bind.

Okay. Let me ask you a question.
Are you a winner?

Babe.

What?

What kind of question is that?

I mean if life is a game.

Life's not a fucking game.

You get on my fucking nerves.

Are you real Micah?

Sit down Noah.

I see you.

Sit down somewhere man.

I hear you.
You don't sound like you.
I don't trust what I see.
I don't trust what I hear.

Gaze

It's a hypothetical, Noah.

I understand what a hypothetical is.

Noah, I don't ask you for a lot.
Answer me.

If you let me…

In this life we have made-
In this life we are making-

Why are you doing this?

Are you a winner?
Are you a loser?

Noah gazes at the shape of Micah.

Are you?

At this moment?

Uh huh.
Sure, at this very moment.

I mean I've lost a lot.
I've gained. Is won the same as gained?

When you add it all fucking up and subtract
or whatever other math you have to do for yourself
to arrive at the number?
You winning or you losing?

Right now?

Yes, Noah.
Right now.

I'd say, I've lost.

I didn't ask you if you've lost.
I asked you whether in this moment
in life
are you a winner or a loser?

I guess- I'm a loser.
I'm a fuckin' loser.

Micah turns from his love.

Micah.
Micah.
Micah!

DISPATCH

bathroom mirror

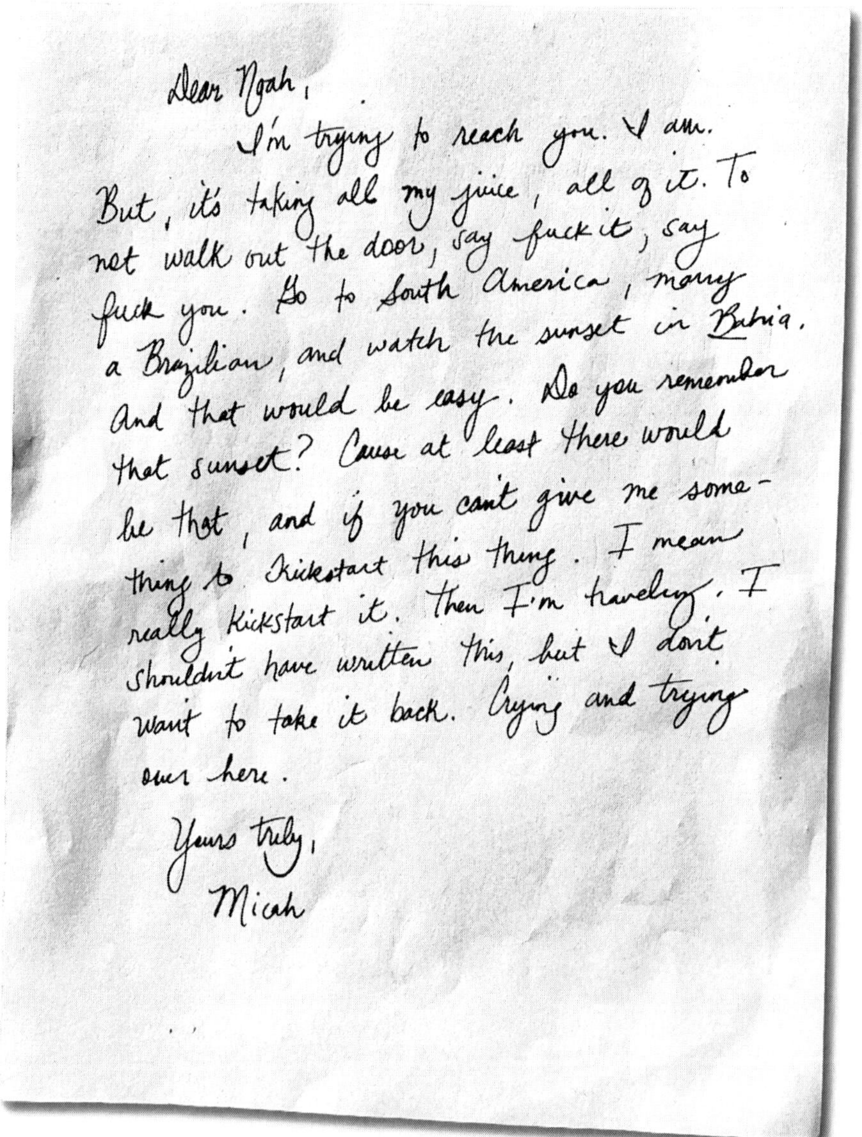

Dear Noah,
I'm trying to reach you. I am.
But, it's taking all my juice, all of it. To
not walk out the door, say fuck it, say
fuck you. Go to South America, marry
a Brazilian, and watch the sunset in Bahia.
And that would be easy. Do you remember
that sunset? Cause at least there would
be that, and if you can't give me some-
thing to kickstart this thing. I mean
really kickstart it. Then I'm traveling. I
shouldn't have written this, but I don't
want to take it back. Crying and trying
over here.

Yours truly,
Micah

SPRING

front door blues

Last night I did something that I swore I never do
Last night I said something I said I'd wasn't gone say.
Open my front door, and let that man have his way.
Opened my front door, and he took my voice away.
Oh -
Oh -
He's -
He's -
He knows -
He can -
Lord -
Baby -

AUTUMN

heart

Where is my heart. Where is my
heart. Where is
my heart. Where
is my heart.
Where is my
heart. Where is
my heart. Where
is my heart.
Where is my
heart. Where is
my heart. Where
is my heart.
Where is my
heart. Where is
my heart. Where
is my heart.
Where is my
heart. Where is
my heart. Where
is my

SPRING

survey

Where I come out
of the woods
the land is flat
no sense
of relief.
You become an expert
in one thing
watching
the horizon

AUTUMN

hold me like the dark

My brother fell.

I found a love.

I picked him up.

Not before.

Before what.

Before you spit on him.

Kicked him.

Told him what you thought about him.

Meaning you judged him.

While you stretched out your hand the whole time.

I found a kiss.

Where'd you find it?

Noah kisses his Love.

I courted you.

You found me.

You were in the fields
dreaming of a way.

Away, where's that at?

I found a love.

Or an argument.

No. No…
Babe, you're a Song.

Behind the church.

FUCKING

In your field.

In your woods.

FUCKING

Yeah. In the cotton.

On the cotton.

Remember the smell?

Oil. Dirt. Reaping.
How did we get here?

You splendid.
Touch me here.

Micah strokes the prosthetic
leg, the carbon fiber
bound by plastic
none of it the color of his own flesh.

Tell me something.

What?

Something from there.
Noah touches the chest of his lover.

Okay…
I got Stacy pregnant when we were in high school.

What? Noah laughs.
No you didn't!

Her Mom took her to have an abortion.
I held her hand in the backseat.
Your turn.

Alright…
I stole a picture of my uncle,
the one that disappeared.

Why?

Some part of me suspected
that I was like him
that I wanted to disappear.

Do you still have it?

I threw it away. I wanted to complete the act for him.

What else?

I got a new rifle.

Micah gazes at his love.

Noah meets his lover's gaze.

Micah places his hand on Noah's chest.
Tell me something from here.

You think you're powerful. You're not. You're just scared.

Noah travels into heart of Silence.

We are on a raid. Outside Mosul.
The sun falls over their eyes,
The mother, the father, the child.
I smell fear.
Not mine. My heart is racing.
I feel. What?
Bad? I feel-
Not bad.
It is only that I think
I should feel
bad. The truth is
I feel giddy.
This feels like power.
Like church in my hands.
We do it the same way
every time.
Run into the room.
Gather the Iraqis in the dark
Orient our weapon.
Some mother
always screams.
This.

You have been waiting
for this
transgression.
The part where you
earn your pay.
Get your spirit
in this dark.
But if your mother named you Noah
you can't share that feeling.
The other soldiers. Them.
I can see them too. Being excited
by the orange sky.
Different and like yours.
Them trying to hide it.
But if you know how to look
You can see.
Right there, behind my eyes.
Inside.
My heart is beating out of my chest
This is the first time.
I craved the danger.
I needed it.
It excited me.
My dick got hard.

And isn't that wrong?
And I see the fear in their eyes
the father , the mother, the child.
And I know that this is wrong
but I can't help it.
I can't.

Do you want to go back Noah?

No - Yes. No.
Sometimes.

Gaze

Come here. Baby.
Hold me.

Micah gazes at the shape of distance.

Can you hold me
like the dark?

No.
I don't think I can.

SPRING

I pray.
On the soldier highways
rusty lean phantom soldiers
with your rucksacks of molten tar
when you slept, I put a glass to your chest
and listened.
Remember, it was me who shipped you away
angered and uncertain.
Remember when you called me an ungrateful child.
At first, I said this freedom has a peal to it—
When you didn't come back
I knew it was an execution.
Phantom soldier
come home.
Noah
reach back to me.

WILDERNESS

commandment

In the dark
Micah bends before Noah's
sleeping body.
Micah places the glass on
his chest.
Micah listens
to Noah's inside.

Thou shalt

What if we

My leg

Misshape

Which comes first

The blast

His leg is a rock

Or the blade

A blade cuts

No exit wound

Maybe the hole started from the inside

We should discuss necrosis

Is it neurosis

Thou shalt not

Rock

Leave

When can he

When can I

Can't. Must not

My leg is a rock

Kill

See the hole that is my leg

Which comes first

When can I

How big was the bomb

Was it a bomb

The door

Was there a tick-tick-tick

What are the parameters of the blast site

Where to mark it

In that place where he keeps the secrets

What about the door

Never mind the door

When can I

Thou shalt

Sometimes explosions are good

When

Where is the blade

Controlled demolitions

The blade is a bomb

Where does the body begin

not kill

and the mind end?

Noah's body wakes.
Noah knocks Micah to the floor.
Glass thuds on the hard wood.

Lovers wrestle in the dark.
Noah's hand closes on Micah's throat.
Micah struggles to breathe.

Noah deep inside
a temple or a wilderness
or a desert
Noah's hand squeezes tighter
around Micah's throat.

Micah reaches for the blade
or the blade finds Micah.
At the threshold of recovery
or the wood
or consciousness
Micah thrusts the blade
into Noah's side.
Noah gasps. Noah bleeds.
Micah breathes.

Ha

SPRING

Micah journeys deepest into the wood.

There
in a copse of dense
cool fern
Micah kneels.

FALL

In the wood
Micah fashions memory into circle.

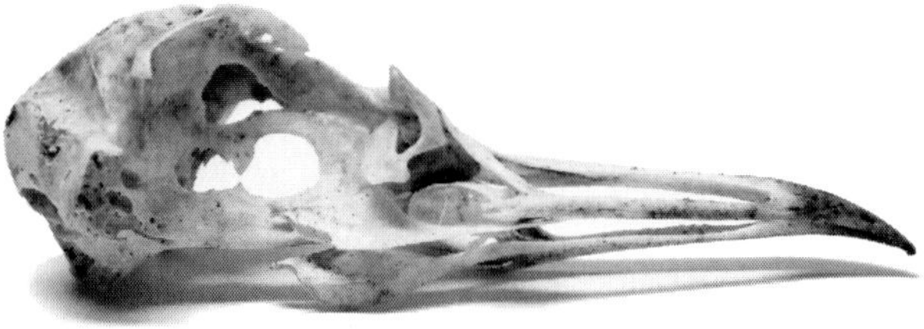

Found in the graveyard beyond the wood, towards the levee.
Praise the silent oath to the living.
Birds sip from the pool.
Let the earth read the sky.

One of my bees found in his drawer in a jar wrapped in a blanket.
WTF
After school, we would go on expeditions, discovering unknown worlds.
I call the multitude. Sound and Work. Beat your wings.

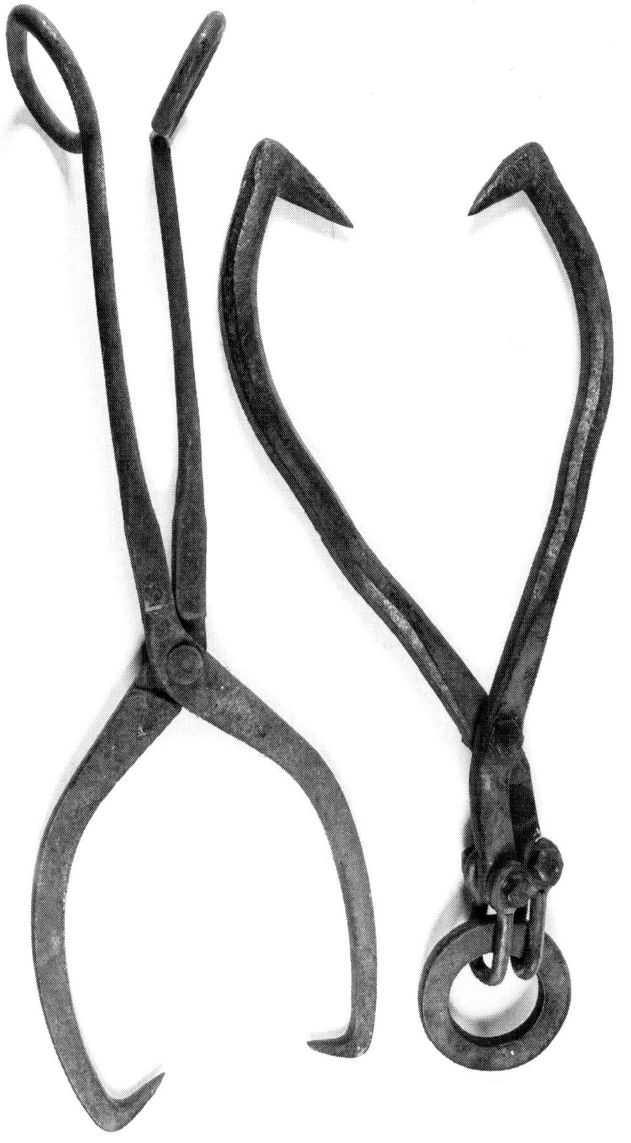

Found at the edge of the north field, closest to the wood.
You were never careful enough with me.
In second grade, you bought us slushies. Held each cup by the tips of your fingers.
I'll pick up your soul. Drag it back. If I have to.

From his pocket.

He obsesses over it. Takes it out of his pocket, when he thinks I'm not watching.

I know it's from the mountain.

Call on the truth of the Mountain. Gnash, and Snarl, and Tear at the Image.

Found on the floorboard of Noah's tractor.

He be on some real caveman shit some time.

We can go anywhere in the world. Any world. So we travel together through every opening beneath the sweetgum. Every dark opening.

I call the dark out of the fruit.

Micah dips and archs and thrashes his body.

Found at John the Conk's Hoodoo Shop.
Shake it all off.
Where we dance atop the thick humid air.
Use the wind. Make a shape from the earth. Spin. Again and Again and Again.

WINTER

possession

Micah calls to Noah
a thousand times.

When the wilderness dispatches the temple and the desert dispatches home and autumn dispatches spring and the field dispatches the wood-

–SHU–
reveals
the worlds.

Possession

Possession

Possession

Possession

Possession

Possession

Possession

He took my heart

He is a thief

Take my soul

He has my voice

Take my body

He takes time

There in the wood
before Micah
the desert
gathers shape.
Micah hones his gaze.

In the desert

Noah advances.
Kill!

The temple opens.

Inside the temple
The soldiers cry out.

Yet forty days and
Nineveh shall be overthrown.

Noah identifies the target.
Center Mass

Micah gazes into the temple.
Mark him!

Noah zeroes in.
Torso

Noah readies his weapon.
Unsling.

Micah gazes
hungry with witness.

Noah's body tightens.
Aluminiumed

Carbined

Verticaled

On back weight.

Inside the temple
The soldiers cry
Kill

Noah readies himself.
Rock and stone.

Cross body weight.

Rock and stone.

Noah hesitates
In hand weight.

Noah gazes across time.
Rock and stone.

Noah calls to his Love.
Help me to bear all uneven weight.
Micah builds a bridge.

And from a great distance, Noah hears the familiar.

Noah
Reach back to me.

There in the wood, Micah gathers sound. Gathers shape. Holds them before him as an image. Micah lowers himself to the ground.

Micah speaks to the ground. Gathers dust. Holds dust with attention.

Count Dust 100…99, 98, 97, Flat barren terrain, desert or tarmac: Flat conditions increase the likelihood of the hot-air "fuel" being a near constant. Dusty or sandy conditions will cause particles to become caught up in the vortex, making the dust devil easily visible.

The dust takes its own shape. Travels across space.

All the Way 79, 78, 77, 76...

Clear skies or lightly cloudy conditions: The surface needs to absorb significant amounts of solar energy to heat the air near the surface and create ideal dust devil conditions.

Travels Across time. On the mountain, to Noah.

15, 14, 13 12

The underlying factor for sustaining the desert tornado is the extreme difference in temperature between the near-surface air and the atmosphere. Windy conditions will destabilize the spinning effect of a desert tornado. Back to Wonder. Light to No Wind and Cool Atmospheric Temperature.

Inside the temple, the word of the Lord came unto Jonah the son of the Amittai, saying

–SHU– catches Micah.

Mount

–SHU–with–Micah watches.

Arise, go to Nineveh, that great city, and cry against it; For their wickedness is come up before me.

36°19'13.9"N 42°35'47.1"E

the mountain speaks

Nineveh

Not Ninevah
Ninevah now Mosul
See the city.

Noah

A man and another.
Noah and another.
A sergeant and Noah.
In contest

measure

their rifles. We know
the way men do.
In this myth
Noah's weapon is

longer.

What a man says is
I carried the weight of a child in Bosnia!

Gather

The sergeant's wild is thicker
I got bodies in Grenada!

the dogs

Shoot them all.
The sergeant commands.

kill not mercy.

Kill.
The sergeant commands.

I TREMBLE

Noah refuses.

I QUAKE

Time is as

LAY YOUR BODY DOWN.

long as silence.

Lay your body down
Noah commands.

And should I not spare Nineveh, that great city, wherein are more than six score persons that cannot discern between their right hand and their left?

On my peak,
the sergeant cannot

move.

Noah retrains
his weapon
center

mass

The sergeant lies
prostrate

before death.

At my base,
the sheepherder
kneels before all

greatness.

Allah

at noon

day time.

Beyond

Them, inside
the city gates.
A new mother
in the house.
marred by small arms

fire.

Inside the same
house with twin fig
trees outside. Mother
sings her new born

a lullaby.

Laila
La-eee-lah.
Who are you?
The mother sings.

Who are you?

Noah screams

Yalla.

The mother sings.

Therefore, I will wail and howl,
I will go stripped and naked,
I will make a wailing like the dragons
and mourning as the owls.

–SHU–with–Micah dances before the temple.

WILDERNESS

Temple

A temple quiets the earth,
When did you return?

I returned.

gathers silence,
More specifically.

I returned 1 year and 6 months, 3 days ago.

compounds that silence.
And were you excited at the prospect of returning home?

I wasn't well.

A temple shaves the bark from time,
Noah, what do you hope to gain here inside?

I need to be better than I am.

hammers the blade,
Is there something more tangible that you want from our time together?

I'd like to sleep.

cools the instrument in fire.
Yes, we always return to sleep.

Temple
suspended in fire.

Noah
suspended in ache.

A temple echoes ache.
About how many hours of sleep do you average a night?

My name?

A temple studies the *Ha*,
Do you think of harming yourself?

Noah.

and heats the blade,
Do you think of harming others?

My name is Noah.

and minds the gate.
Do you experience hallucinations?

My name is Noah.

A temple factors the earth.
Do you hear voices?

Micah calls.

A temple reschedules the flesh.
Do you think about the future?

Micah will come for me.

A temple reappoints the spirit.
It might mean going into the desert.

Back to Iraq.

A temple burns the grassy field.
Another kind of Iraq.

Back to Mosul.

A temple reappoints the flesh.
There are other deserts, you know.

Back to Mississippi.

A temple weeps for its silence.
Some deserts that have always been with us.

My take.

A temple mouths the written.
Does Micah find you?

The voice thins.

A temple mocks Time.
Why can't you call to him?

I fix
my mind
to say a thing.
My mind
turns
from the word.
What comes
out of my mouth
is not
the thing
I know
in my mind.
What comes is my take.

A temple examines the blade.
Has your "take" always been with you?

At night in bed.
I dream about killing Micah.

A temple praises the dream.
It is a dream Noah.

And he looks at me.

His gaze peels flesh

from my bones.

A temple waits for the morning.
Is it guilt you feel?

Guilt?

A temple inquires of justice.
If I ask you.

A temple explodes laughter.
If I tell you I need you.

A temple shakes the edifice.
If I beg.

Will you stay?

Noah journeys into the heart of the desert.

Temple cries out in the wilderness.

Where the desert gazes at
the wilderness and home
gazes at the temple and the
field gazes at the wood and
autumn gazes at spring-

Micah–with–SHU–with–Noah
opens the
worlds.

Noah digs in the desert.

Capture.
Release.
Dig and Hold.

The night sky burns orange.

Capture.
Release.
Dig and Hold.

Sand pours through his hands.

Capture.
Release.
Dig and—

Noah spits into sand.
Noah fashions
a leg.

Capture. Hold and—

Noah stands.
The wind blows.
The leg
fails.

Capture. Release.

Dig and Hold.

Noah weeps.

Release. Hold.

Tears fall into
sand.

Capture. Hold.

Noah fashions a leg in the
desert.

Capture. Capture and—

The leg fails.

Release. Hold.

The night sky burns
orange.

Capture.

Noah digs and
pisses into sand
fashions leg from
sand.

Hold and—

Noah stands erect.

The leg fails.

Release and—

Noah thrashes and wails
and digs
through sand
through memory
and suddenly sandstone.

Dig and Hold.

Noah digs and digs
through stone.
Noah frees
mastodon and brachiopod
and trilobite.

Capture. Hold.

Noah fashions a leg from
stone.
The stone burns
orange.

Release and—

Noah fastens the leg
to his body.
Noah lowers
his ear to the stone
listens.

Hold and—

Beneath stone
a rushing river.
Noah digs
an opening.

Dig.

Mastadon and brachiopod
and trilobite

fall out from stone
into river.
Noah gazes.

Noah dives down into
the water.
Cool.
Noah's leg burns
orange.

Capture. Release.

Mastadon and brachiopod
and trilobite
encircle Noah.

Hold and—

Noah sinks
from the weight of
the stone leg.

Dig and—

The creatures
swim and gaze
upon Noah.

Capture and—

Beneath them,
an eddy
pulls the stone
pulls Noah
down.

Release and—

Noah sinks.
Noah swims harder.
Noah sinks
deeper
and deeper

Capture.
Release.
Dig and Hold.

Spinning
on the rim of the eddy
Noah struggles
to unfasten the leg.

Dig and Dig
and Dig and—

Noah spins.
Noah unfastens the leg.

Dig and—

The eddy swallows
the leg.

Dig.

Noah
creature among creatures
swims and swims.
Buoyant
Noah's body burns
orange.

The image fades before Micah–with–SHU– which is a way into the words which is a way into the worlds which is a way into the World.

–SHU– departs from Micah.

Micah returns to his body.
Ice falls onto the wood.
Outside the circle
hours pass
limbs hang
heavy
trees crack
weighted with water
darkness falls.
A thousand ospreys
sing the living.
Trees crack.
Hours pass.
A thousand times a thousand deer
huddle for warmth.
Inside the circle
Micah keeps vigil
extends his limbs.
Ice falls
and falls
and
the sun rises
orange
and
the ice melts
and the trees
crack and crack
and
the worlds gazes
upon Micah.

DISPATCH

apiary

Dear Micah,

I felt you against my chest last night. Please don't invade my space. From past events, we know that we need to be more careful when I sleep. Of course, it was not my intention to strangle you. Luckily you're strong. Maybe, I am really angry and it only surfaces when I'm asleep. I honestly don't know. You say that I'm not trying but I am... I need you to see that.

What I know is, when I wake up, sometimes I don't feel much. I know this isn't what you want to hear, but that cold glass, you put on my chest hurts me Micah. Stop trying to look at my insides. And while I would rather say these things to your face, I do see the effectiveness of writing it all down. You can't hear my heart Micah, of course I don't think it's here.

I'm writing this letter because I do remember what it was like before. So unless we are awake, please stay on your side of the bed. And so for now, I'll just keep going through the motions. Love — Noah

P.S. I'll start taking the Viagra again, but sometimes it makes me hurl.

BEGIN AGAIN

END

END

BEGIN AGAIN